"What's wrong with him?" Laura shouted.

"I don't know," Grant answered, obviously agitated. "Maybe he just woke up to find himself lying in a drawer with a couple of giant strangers standing over him. Hell, *I'd* scream."

Laura wrung her hands. "Oh my God, what are we going to do?"

"Panic's good," Grant complained, still holding the child out in front of him as if the baby were a live hand grenade...with the pin already pulled. "Here—" He transferred Tucker to Laura's arms. "You try. Maybe he wants his mother."

Laura jostled and rocked the little boy, but Tucker only screamed louder and pushed against her. "Take him. He hates me," she cried frantically as she juggled struggling baby limbs.

Grant swiftly drew the screaming little boy into his arms, then held him to his heart, rocking him. And this time...it worked. The baby instantly quieted.

"It's true. He does hate—"

"Shhh!" Grant warned, waving a hand at her from under the baby's bottom. "Look—" He pointed with that same hand. "He's almost asleep."

Darned if he wasn't right. The baby actually seemed to like Grant. *So where did that leave her?*

Dear Reader,

I have some very exciting news! In May of this year, we are launching a great new series called Harlequin Duets.

Harlequin Duets will offer two brand-new novels in one book for one low price. You will continue enjoying wonderful romantic comedy-type stories from more of the authors you've come to love! The two Harlequin Duets novels to be published every month will each contain two stories, creating four wonderful reading experiences each month. We're bringing you twice as much fun and romance with Harlequin Duets!

This month Cheryl Anne Porter delights us with *FROM HERE TO MATERNITY*, part of our Right Stork, Wrong Address miniseries. Up-and-coming ad exec Laura Sloan is in over her head when she finds an abandoned baby in her office, *and* her first love on her doorstep. Suddenly she's got two males to contend with—and she hasn't got a clue what to do with either one of them! Also out this month is Lois Greiman's dangerously funny *HIS BODYGUARD*. It's not very often a macho hero is forced to hire a female bodyguard. Watch the fireworks as Nathan Fox is charmed and captivated by petite, curvaceous Brittany O'Shay—and deeply chagrined when she does, in fact, save his life.

Once again, I hope you enjoy Love & Laughter. And don't forget to look for Harlequin Duets, on sale in April!

Humorously yours,

Malle Vallik

Malle Vallik
Associate Senior Editor

FROM HERE TO MATERNITY
Cheryl Anne Porter

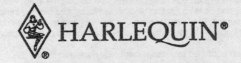

HARLEQUIN®

TORONTO • NEW YORK • LONDON
AMSTERDAM • PARIS • SYDNEY • HAMBURG
STOCKHOLM • ATHENS • TOKYO • MILAN • MADRID
PRAGUE • WARSAW • BUDAPEST • AUCKLAND

ISBN 0-373-44063-4

FROM HERE TO MATERNITY

A funny thing happened...

Harlequin could not have picked a better time to ask me to write a story with a baby in it. My precious baby grandson, T.J., had just participated as a model in a photo shoot for a nationwide ad campaign. And, as the star-in-training's grandmother, I tagged along. As I watched T.J. and all the other babies being...well, babies, and the adults being...well, completely unstrung as the day wore on, an idea came to me. A really funny idea—especially since my friend was the VP ad exec in charge of the shoot. A single, childless VP ad exec, I might add, who ended up offering the tiny tots large sums of money and fancy cars to cooperate.

They say that truth is stranger than fiction, and with children involved, it can get pretty strange. And funny. I hope this story makes you chuckle (but not too loudly, you'll wake the baby).

Cheryl Anne Porter

To T.J. Porter, my little star baby.
And to all the fun people at Curtin and Pease.
You know who you are!

1

"YOU'RE NOT going to like this, boss. We have a problem."

Laura tensed, her insides curdling with dread. She looked up from the clutter on her desk to see David, her hotshot, five-years-younger-than-her creative director, standing in the doorway...and grinning. Never a good sign. She sighed and stood up. "Is it a Grant Maguire problem?"

"No." He followed this with a frown and added, "Well, not exactly..." Laura started to bolt. "Wait! He's not here," David promised, his hand raised. Laura flopped onto her seat and sent David her best baleful expression. His grin returned. "Come on, Laura, what gives? You've had Maguire's account for a month. And you've avoided him from day one. I mean, he *is* the new marketing director for Tucker the Bear. How long do you think you can keep dodging him?"

Laura's shrug accentuated her determination—okay, irrational stubbornness—on the Grant Maguire issue. "How long is eternity?"

David chuckled. "Eternity. Wow. You *really* don't want to see him."

"No. And I *really* don't want to talk about him, either." Laura realized she was sulking, a very un-advertising-executive thing to do. She sucked her bottom lip in and tried to look suitably threatening.

It was lost on David. He raised his hands in an

I-give-you-win gesture, then laughed. "Fine. You're the boss. It's refreshing to see at least one female around here who isn't praying to catch just one more glimpse of him."

Laura tried to act flippant. "Yeah, well, give him his due. Not every guy makes the cover of *Celebrity* magazine as the world's most eligible bachelor."

"And here you can't get away from him fast enough."

A grin—Laura feared a sickly one—reflected her somersaulting emotions. "Call me crazy."

David shook his head. "I don't think so. You can cause my checks not to be signed."

Laura couldn't help chuckling at that. "So, David, what *is* this 'not exactly a Grant Maguire problem'? And by the way, whatever it is, I already hate him—it. The problem."

"Not as much as you're going to," David assured her as he crossed her office and slouched comfortably on one of the leather-upholstered chairs facing her desk. Apparently he hadn't caught her him-it slip. She knew the turkey would've called her on it. "So. Are you busy?"

"Are you kidding?" Laura stared at him and then dramatically slumped over her desk. With her cheek pressed against her work and her hair covering her face, her words were muffled. "Ad proofs. Media schedules. Marketing plans. Client files. Art boards. All needing approval *yesterday,* David. But no, I'm not busy. And it is *only* six o'clock."

"All right. I get it."

"Good. So, how big is this problem?"

"Baby size."

Laura lay there a second, thinking and blinking, and then sat up, shoving her hair back and staring at David.

"Baby size…as in it's a little problem, not a giant problem? Or baby size as in a problem with a baby?"

"B. A problem with a baby."

Laura stiffened, gripping the edge of her desk, again ready to jump up and jet out the door. "Why are we sitting here discussing Grant Maguire if something's wrong with one of the models? Talk to me. Problem how? Problem hurt? Problem missing?" Like neon signs, her thoughts flashed, *Lawsuit, lawsuit.*

"Relax. Not hurt. Not missing," David answered.

She relaxed…some. "Okay. Good. But I thought all the babies and their parents went home." When David didn't answer, dread filled Laura. "David, tell me they all went home."

He shrugged. "Can't. There's still one here. No mama. No papa. No note. The talent agency says he's not theirs. We have no release on him. Steve doesn't remember taking shots of him. No one saw him come in. Or get carried in, I guess, since he doesn't look to be more than eight or nine months old. Anyway, he's just here. Him and his infant carrier. And we don't know why."

Frozen in place, Laura gripped the armrests of her chair and stared at David as long and wordless moments passed. "My stomach hurts."

"It's supposed to," David assured her. "It comes with the title on your door." He pointed to the Vice President etched into the brass plate there.

Laura ignored him. "Just how did this baby thing happen?"

"Beats me. I guess in all the craziness, with eight babies and their mothers here all day for the Tucker the Bear photo shoot, someone just slipped in with him…and then left. Pretty cold, huh?"

"Yeah. I'd say. David, this is awful."

"I know. Who'd do something like this?"

"Somebody desperate, no doubt. Where is he now? The baby, I mean."

"With Michelle. In her office. But she has to go, so she sent me to get you. Something about her wedding dress or the cake. It doesn't fit or doesn't taste good. Who knows? Anyway, she's in a full-blown bride tizzy."

Laura grimaced. "Great. Anything else I should know?"

"Yeah. But I can't tell you. Because it's one of those you-have-to-see-it-to-believe-it things."

Laura exhaled loudly. "David, you've heard about my family. My entire life has to be seen to be believed. So just tell me what it is."

"Uh-uh. Nice try." David chuckled. "Gotta see it to believe it, boss."

Laura wrinkled her nose. "Fine. Then we'd better get down there." She stood. David followed suit. Then, from out of nowhere—well, maybe from somewhere deep inside Laura's secret self—came a wistful thought. "Michelle's wedding. That poor kid. The whole thing is making her nuts. I'm just glad—for her—that it's in a few weeks. I know if it was me, I'd elope and be done with it."

I'd elope and be done with it? Me? Married? Ha! But an unguarded emotion accompanied Laura's denial and clutched at her heart, forcing her to be honest with herself. Lately—okay, Grant-back-in-her-professional-life lately—she'd found her thoughts...well, lingering on Michelle's upcoming wedding. Did she, Laura Elizabeth Sloan, want all those things, too? The excitement. *Grant.* Love. *Grant.* A promise of fulfillment. *Grant.* Someone to share her life with. *Grant.* The prospect of a family. *With Grant.* Sex. *With Grant.*

Sighing, almost unaware that she had, Laura's gaze drifted to the picture window behind David. He turned, too, apparently interpreting her flash of solemnity as weather worry. "Looks nasty, huh?"

"Yes. It does," Laura murmured. And she was right. It did. Heavy gray clouds crept over Manhattan's late Tuesday afternoon, jagged, building-punctured skyline. Then again, and unbidden, she returned to her thoughts of Grant. Of commitments. And forevers. And...every wonderful thing she could never have with him. That was the *real* reason she'd been avoiding the man. Why, after all, *why* should she subject herself to the torture of seeing him and of loving— *Stop it, Laura.*

Yes. Stop it. She stiffened, trying to put out of her mind how the thought that Grant was back in her life, even if only professionally, moved her soul, stirred her heart...and made her body ache for him. For his touch. In fact, if she sat back and relaxed a moment, if she thought back to her college days, ten years gone, she was almost sure she could feel his hands on her, stroking her skin, his mouth moving over her... Laura jerked to the moment. Her eyes widened. Her heart pounded. What was she doing?

Fearing her inner lustings may have shown on her face, Laura glanced at David. He stared at the approaching weather. Laura exhaled, relaxed and forced her Grant yearning to its tiny little pigeonhole in her mind. Filed it under Don't Even Think About It. Then she directed her professional attention to David. "All right, down to business. We can't keep a baby here. So, what do we do with it?"

David raised his eyebrows. "We? Oh, no. I'm not the VP ad exec. You are. Cohn and Draper pays *you* the big bucks. Not me. I'm just the messenger. So...see ya, hate to be ya." He crossed her office with a stiff-legged, determined stride. He rounded the corner and made for the long hall that led to Nancy at the front desk and the bank of elevators across from her.

Only then did the fact that he was wearing his overcoat imprint itself on Laura's consciousness. The man was bailing. Laura called out, "Oh, no, you don't. Get back here." But he didn't. Already up and skirting her desk, Laura chased after him. "Don't leave me here with a baby. They're not safe around me. My own mother wouldn't leave my brothers and sisters with me, David. Our baby-sitter used to be the people at nine-one-one. Wait!"

But he didn't. He did, however, call over his shoulder, "Don't worry about it. You're a female. It should come naturally."

"But it won't," Laura yelled, stopping outside her office, refusing to participate in an undignified chase down the hall. From the doorway, she insisted—rather loudly—"I hurt little kids."

As if on cue, doors up and down the corridor opened. And out poured Cohn and Drapers' finest. All homeward bound and downright shocked as they stopped and stared Laura's Tucker the Bear baby-products account-executive way. A furious heat of embarrassment flushed Laura's cheeks, made all the worse, she knew, by her fair Irish complexion.

"Well...I don't *hurt* them. Not on purpose..." She immediately began dissembling. "Hurt's probably not the right word, anyway. Accident is. Yes. Accident. Things just happen with me and kids." She began backing into her office. "Of course, that whole toilet thing with my sister was just that, an accident. And her foot healed. How she got it stuck in there, I don't know. We were— Well, it's not important. Besides, you'd hardly notice her limp today."

Safely over the threshold, Laura firmly closed the door in her own face. And then she stood there, staring at it. The way she saw it, she had two choices. Live out the remainder of her life behind this closed door. Or open it and face the world. *Okay. Door number two.* Taking a deep breath, she gripped the doorknob, turned it, opened the door and strode down the emptying hallway, executively in control and determined to get to the bottom of this.

"You're a female. It should come naturally." Ha. As *if*, she fumed as she wandered through the agency's hallways until she arrived at Michelle's office.

Blond, slender, softly feminine, Michelle sat with her back to the doorway, totally engrossed with an infant carrier, in which—Laura took two carpet-muffled steps to her right—resided an infant. A black-haired, blue-eyed bundle of...what had David said? A boy? Laura checked the baby's outfit. Yep, a boy, judging by its—his—blue sleeper with a...

Laura gasped. She knew what David's "something you have to see to believe" was. Tucker the Bear. The baby had a Tucker the Bear logo on the front of his clothes. Grant Maguire's new Tucker the Bear design. Not the old one. The *new* one that was still and only an artist's rendering on her desk. One that hadn't been perfected yet, much less approved. A prototype that wasn't on clothing, in stores, at factories or adorning *anything* yet.

Except this baby's sleeper. So here she was, staring at a virtual impossibility. Because she and her team had just come up with the design a week ago and were still in the process of checking it against all licenses. And she hadn't even run it by the client—again, Grant Maguire—yet. So how'd—?

Wait a minute. Laura narrowed her eyes in a squint

of confusion even as a chill ran over her skin. What was going on here? Was this someone's idea of a joke? And who was this kid? Or better yet, whose kid was he? Laura lowered her hand, focusing her gaze on the child. The baby in question was grinning and chortling at Michelle. No wonder. She was cooing and tickling him and saying, "Hey, little sweetie. How are you, huh? Where's your mommy?"

As luck or cruel fate would have it, at that instant the baby turned to Laura, waving a chubby fist in her direction...as if to name her as his parent. As yet unnoticed by Michelle, Laura flitted out of view and gave in to a weak and sweaty feeling. *This is not happening,* she firmly told herself. *When I step back inside, that baby and his Tucker the Bear will be gone, and none of this will be happening.*

Laura resolutely stepped back inside. Not only was the cherubic little boy still there, but he was again looking at her, his blue eyes clear and alert. He blinked and smiled and waved his arms animatedly. Apparently noticing the direction of the baby's gaze, Michelle pivoted, saw Laura and smiled. "Hey, there you are."

"No, I'm not," Laura assured her...then heard herself. "Well, I mean, yes I am here. Only I'm not his mother."

Michelle pulled back, chuckling, giving Laura a what's-wrong-with-you look. "Well, who didn't know that? We all know how much *you* like babies," she teased.

Laura's face heated with guilt. "I avoid them for their own safety, Michelle. They're just better off not being anywhere in my vicinity, trust me."

"Oh, please. I don't believe all those wild stories you tell about growing up with all those brothers and sisters." When Laura grinned and shrugged, Michelle rolled her eyes at her boss. Then she turned to the little boy in the carrier and pointed at him. "Isn't he adorable? He's the sweetest little guy. And look. He's wearing the new Tucker the Bear design."

Laura was frowning when Michelle turned her way. Her art director's light brown eyes were questioning. "Did I miss a meeting, Laura? I mean, how *did* this logo get on here? The last I heard, we hadn't even gotten client approval. And yet here it is."

Laura managed to nod. "I know. I see it. But there were no meetings. No decisions. So I don't know what to think, either."

Michelle's expression darkened. "Wow. Then this is really weird, isn't it?"

"Exceptionally. If not cosmically," Laura quickly agreed, crossing her arms under her bosom.

A wordless moment passed, then Michelle brightened, smiling at her. "Want to hold him?"

Laura backed up, waving Michelle's request away. "No, thank you. I've been holding spewing babies for the last two days of the photo shoot. And no one got hurt. Which is something of a victory for me. So I think I'll just stop while the only casualty is my wet-wipe of a suit."

Michelle laughed. "In that case, what's one more stain? Come on. Hold him." With that, she unstrapped the baby and picked him up, holding him under his arms and kissing his fat little cheek. For all her kind efforts, though, the baby grabbed a handful of Michelle's blond hair and yanked it hard, right before stuffing her curls into his little round mouth. Michelle's squeal of dismay galvanized Laura into action.

She quickly squatted next to Michelle, taking the baby's hand and trying, as gently as possible, to pry his fat little fingers open. He immediately cooperated, releasing Michelle's hair and grabbing Laura's finger, gripping it tightly and saying mama with a disconcerting note of certainty in his baby voice.

Laura all but passed out. Desperately she waggled her finger, still held hostage in his fat ones, and managed to quip, "Hey, I'm not Mama. Don't you know that's how rumors get started?"

Michelle's chuckle, as she massaged her scalp, told Laura that she'd sounded as droll as she thought she had. Immediately, Laura's face heated with self-consciousness. To deflect it, she changed the subject. "It looks like you've done a great job of caring for him here, Michelle."

"It wasn't hard. He sat there in his little carrier, happy as a clam, and stared out the door. Like he was expecting someone." Her face softened with sympathy. "Probably his mother, poor baby. Anyway, I didn't do anything you wouldn't." Then she brightened some. "Heck, you probably would have done a better job, given that big family of yours."

"Not mine. My mother's. And, trust me, there is no 'better job' when it comes to me and kids," Laura assured her. But still, she couldn't stop a chuckle as she thought of her wonderfully crazy and exasperating gypsy of a mother, her five marriages, five relocations and her five children to prove each one. "Even though I'm the oldest, my mother knew better than to let me help with the babies," Laura added. "So I know nothing about the diaper crowd. Okay, not even about the curtain-climber set. Anyway, my shaving the right half of James's head the day before school pictures were to be taken seemed to be the last straw for my mother."

"You what?" Michelle squealed. "Laura Sloan! That's awful. You *shaved* his head? Why?"

Grinning wickedly, Laura shrugged. "He said he wanted a haircut. So I gave him one. Well, half a one."

Her mouth open, Michelle said, "I cannot believe you did that. How old were you then?"

Staring at the baby, Laura frowned, thinking back to the incident. "I guess I was about nine or ten. And James was six. But I was totally excused from child care after that. It's a shame, too, because I really do love kids."

"Yeah. It sounds like it," Michelle responded with a shake of her head.

"But I do," Laura protested—over Michelle's laughter. Grinning, Laura focused on the baby and cooed, "Don't I? I love kids. And aren't you the cute little man? Who'd just drop you off, huh? Where's your mama?"

Again, the little boy stared at her, then raised his fist toward her and said, as plain as you please, "Mama." Then he promptly tried to stuff her fingertip into his mouth, and managed to show three or four sharp baby teeth into the bargain.

"Oh, how cute. I think he likes you," Michelle crooned, breaking into the tender moment. "So that means—" she plopped the chubby little guy onto Laura's lap and stood, brushing her woolen slacks "—I can go now. I have to go by the church—"

"No!" Laura bleated. Wrapping an arm around the baby's middle, Laura freed her finger from his clutches and grabbed Michelle's pants, holding her in place. "Stay. Please. I'll give you a thousand dollars not to leave him here with me. Haven't you heard anything I said? Think, Michelle. You're leaving him here with me. With *me*."

"Oh, stop it," Michelle said, laughter bubbling in her

voice. "You're not going to hurt him. You were just a kid yourself back then. You didn't mean to—"

"Ha. Kid? I accidentally left my baby sister in an elevator, Michelle. Five years ago. She was one. I was twenty-five." Hearing her admission, Laura blinked and upped the ante. "I'd better make it two thousand. Have you no pity for this child?"

Michelle laughed outright. "He won't need any. Now, stop it. You'll be fine. He's a good baby."

"*He* may be good, Michelle. But I'm not. I don't know what to do. Seriously. Five minutes after you leave, he could be dangling from the ceiling fan."

Michelle's smile could only be called beatific. "Oh, you. You are so funny." Then she patted Laura's hand, which was still attached to her slacks. "It'll come to you. After all, you're a woman. Mothering is in your genes."

Laura scoffed. "Is this national Mothering Is in Your Genes Day? David said the same thing. Will no one listen to me?" She relinquished her hold on her art director and stared at her. "I'm telling you, it's *not* in my genes. And that's according to my own mother—who should know. And so should you. You've seen me with kids. Admit it. Your hair stood up, didn't it?"

Michelle sobered, looked pensive. "Well, at that one photo shoot a while back, you did give that four-year-old girl five dollars and a subway token to go eat out when her mother said she was hungry."

"See what I mean? This child—" Laura waved the baby's soft, fat little arm at Michelle "—is not safe with me." Then, buoyed by Michelle's stated concern, Laura continued. "Think of it this way, Michelle. Unless Tucker here is somebody's idea of a joke, we have an abandoned baby on our hands. We need to tell someone."

"You mean like Mr. Cohn and Mr. Draper—who are in Switzerland, as we speak? *You're* the someone, Laura. Senior VP on the premises. Everyone else has gone home."

"They have? I am?" Laura's mind whirled with her responsibilities. Liabilities. Lawsuit potential. Career up in smoke. *Think, Laura.* Then she had it. "All right, we should be calling the police or the lost baby people— what are they called?"

Michelle shrugged, frowning as if in thought but glancing toward her coat and purse draped over a chair. "I don't know. Child Protective Services? Child Welfare? Something like that."

Laura smiled brightly. "Yes, that's them. Look them up and we'll call them. Protective. I like that. They sound like people who'll know what to do with someone like...." *Like who?* She glanced at the active bundle on her lap, tugged her gold serpentine-chain necklace from his grasp and looked at Michelle. "What should we call him? I mean, he seems a little young for hey, you or kid."

"Yeah, you're right." Michelle quirked her mouth, looking the baby up and down, then her expression brightened. "I know—how about Tucker? You called him that a minute ago, anyway."

A frown of surprise clouded Laura's features. "I did?" But then she considered the name, the baby—and liked it. "All right, then, Tucker it is."

Laura smiled, suddenly feeling better. They'd call the protective people and have them come get the baby. And then she and Michelle could go home. There. Done. With no loss to her dignity. Well, except that she was still squatting on the floor, holding... *Oh, no.*

A slightly less than dry Tucker, if the warmth spreading over her navy designer suit skirt was any indication.

Laura lifted the baby, stared at the darkly wet circle where he'd been sitting, and her expression crumpled. She held Tucker out to Michelle. "Take him. He's wet."

Not the best opening statement, apparently. Because the art director formerly known as cooperative balked, shaking her head and backing up, stopping only when she got to her coat, which she promptly snatched and shrugged into. "I'd like to help you, but I need to get to the church on time." She grabbed her purse and went the long way around her drafting table, thus avoiding Laura's grasp as she made her way to her door and slipped out. From the hallway she called, "See you tomorrow."

"Not if I see you first," Laura called back. Was she going to have to kill her entire team? And then she was alone with the baby. Quiet moments ticked by while she eyed Tucker and he eyed her.

Then he broke the stalemate. He grinned and reached out, working his little hands and saying, "Mama."

"Yikes. Boy, have you got the wrong girl," Laura said. Still squatting flat-footed, still holding the dangling baby in front of her, her elbows braced on her knees, Laura told him how it was in her life. "Everything else aside, kiddo—and I mean all those horror stories you might have heard, which, by the way, try not to be too freaked out about them, okay? I'll do my best not to drop you on your head or anything— But what I'm trying to say is I'm not the mama kind. I don't even intend to get married."

An unbidden, unwanted image—Grant Maguire's face—flitted into Laura's consciousness. She blinked, dispelling it from her mind. If only it were that easy with her heart. "But, anyway, the boring details aside, I got over him—no! *That.* I got over that, the wanting to get married, a long time ago. I'm happily single. See, look around you, Tucker. This is my life. Glass and chrome. High-rises. City streets. Nightlife. You may not know it, what with me squatted here and serving as your potty chair, but I've made a great life for myself. I make an obscene amount of money. And I'm what we big people call a high-powered executive—''

"Mama." He smiled, pointing at her with a drool-sticky finger.

Laura chuckled as her heart warmed. Why'd he have to be so darned suitable-for-framing cute? "No. *Not* mama. So not mama, you wouldn't believe it, buddy. In fact, you'd run...well, you would if you could. Anyway, try saying this...ex-ec-u-tive. Can you say that?"

"Executive."

Laura froze, staring wide-eyed at the grinning baby. He hadn't said it. No. The husky male voice had come from behind them. Her heart thudding, her limbs tingling, Laura swallowed and came slowly to her feet. Only then, and with great dread pounding her blood through her veins, did she turn around, unthinkingly sticking Tucker under her arm like a quarterback would a football. The child's head and arms hung out one way, his wet bottom and feet the other. With his mouth, he was making rude but happy noises, totally entertaining himself.

However, Laura all but forgot Tucker as she stared at the man leaning against the doorjamb. And he stared at her, appearing to Laura to be just as frozen in place as she felt, just as unwilling to break the moment. Or their eye contact. Their first eye contact in ten years.

Grant Maguire. In the ensuing quiet, images flitted through Laura's mind, reminding her of that fine autumn day on campus years ago when she'd first seen him. She'd fallen in love almost instantly, perhaps loving more the vulnerable little boy she found hidden beneath the Big Man on Campus exterior. She'd thought, in her undergrad days, that he had fallen for her, too. Because their time together had been oh, so torrid. After two years, there'd even been talk of marriage. And that was when the rich as Croesus, handsome as Adonis Golden Boy had bailed. She hadn't seen or heard from him since.

Until now. Here he was. Her client. The heretofore and studiously avoided newly hired marketing director for Tucker the Bear baby products. That he had a job—any job at all—told her he was still into that whole trying-to-prove-himself-to-his-father phase. "Hello, Grant," she finally managed to squeak out around the blush that fired her cheeks.

"Hello, Laura. You're been avoiding me."

She swallowed. "Have not."

"Have to. Either that, or you've been out of the office or in a meeting straight through for the past month."

Her chin came up an embarrassed notch. "Yes, I have."

"Have not." Grant chuckled, the sound causing every nerve ending Laura owned to tingle. Darn it, it just wasn't fair that after ten years, the sound of his voice, of his laugh, should have her wanting to run into his arms. Had she no pride? She'd feared she'd have this weak-kneed, willy-nilly response to him. That was why she'd avoided him. But all that aside, she desperately needed to say something. "So, Grant. You look…good. I guess. I mean, you do. You look good. Better than you do on TV. And in the tabloids. With all those women." *Shut up, Laura.*

Laughter erupted from him. "Thanks…I think. So do you. Look good, I mean."

Her heart leaped. Almost without thought, she shifted the baby's weight on her hip. "I do?"

"Yes. You do."

"Um, thanks." Then it got quiet again. Too quiet. Laura couldn't seem to make herself do or say anything. How could she? Because with all that light brown sun-streaked hair, tawny eyes and tanned skin, even in January, Grant Maguire was—*oh, my God*—standing there. Muscled, lean, fit, the son of one of the richest men in the world. And dressed like a model on the glossy pages of some expensive menswear magazine.

But clothes on him were an afterthought, an unnecessary adornment. Especially since Laura knew what lay underneath them. She didn't have to fantasize. She had firsthand experience. Hands? Her hands. On him. *Oh, my God.* A tingle raced over Laura, centering itself low in her belly. Her breath caught. She stared at him.

He was staring at her. *Crash!* Back to Earth. Back to reality. And back to her appearance. Her soul cringed. *Great. A month of avoiding him, and he catches me like this.* As if she needed to further humiliate herself, Laura saw herself through his eyes. Skirt wet. Hair skewed. Baby in tow. And her a moment ago squatting and talking to the baby. About her life. Her life *alone*. Suddenly, a fit of embarrassed temper replaced Laura's fascination for the man. "How long have you been standing there?" she blurted.

2

"LONG ENOUGH," Grant assured Laura, even though he'd only been there a second or two. He walked into the office, shoving his fisted hands into his overcoat's deep pockets. But he'd been there long enough to know it was either do that—pocket his hands—or risk them reaching out of their own volition to grab her to him for a soul-searing kiss. Totally unexpected.

Unexpected? This bam-right-between-the-eyes, gut-deep wrenching that had his muscles locking and his throat all but closing was merely unexpected? *And the Grand Canyon is just a big ditch, Grant.* All right, certainly he'd expected to have some sort of reaction upon seeing her. After all, he had insisted his company use her agency for their advertising once he heard her name around his office, once he knew she worked here. And that was when his pursuit had started.

He couldn't explain it. He'd thought of her often enough over the years and had thought of looking her up sometime. He'd instinctively realized he still harbored strong feelings for her, but he'd never acted on them. He couldn't really say why. Perhaps it was due to the shame he felt over the way he'd left. But then, hearing her name spoken at work, her A-1 reputation touted, flipped some kind of switch in his head. Or his heart. He'd known somehow that it was time. He needed to see her. To hear her voice. To touch her.

And now here she was. And here he was. The two of them. Staring at each other...for a little too long. Too quiet...for a little too long. Okay, so he hadn't suspected this overtly sexual shock he'd experienced as he watched her from the doorway. How could he have known everything in him would want her, would cry out what a jackass he'd been, would demand that he kiss her, that he beg her to forgive the stupid, idiotic twenty-two-year-old he'd been ten years ago when he left? Beg her to give him a second chance?

And on top of it all, just look at her. Man, she looked good. Tall. Curvy. So womanly. Gone was the untried, gawky young girl he'd fallen in love with. Here was the realization of the woman. So together. Well, together except—and again, no surprise here—for the dangling, chortling baby and the wet skirt and the mussed hair. But still, leave it to her to pull off the patently ridiculous with sexy style. Finally, figuring he'd stood there long enough like some kind of a drooling idiot, Grant pointed to the as yet unremarked upon baby precariously perched under her arm. "What you got there?"

Laura started, as if the sound of his voice had pulled her out of deep thought. She glanced at her bundle. "Um, it appears to be a wet baby."

Grant chuckled, loving the challenging glint in her gray eyes when she looked his way. "I see that. Is he one of ours?"

Laura's eyebrows rose. "Define 'ours.'"

"Tucker the Bear. Baby model. My product, your account? Ours?"

"Oh." Then she shook her head. "No."

Frowning, Grant considered her, not knowing what to make of her ruffled demeanor. Could she be undone because he had the same effect on her as she did on him? Dare he hope as much? But when the moments again stretched out, so did a sudden dread. He had to ask. Had to know. "Well…is he yours, then?"

"Mine?" She said it as if she'd never heard the word.

Grant steeled himself to hear the truth. Where there were babies, there generally were daddies. Husband daddies. "Yes. As in, 'you mama, he son.'"

"No. Oh, God, no. No. He's not mine."

"He's not? Good." Grant heard his blurted reaction at the same moment she did. His eyes widened. "I mean—"

"No. Seriously. It is good. For his sake." She pointed to the baby and put her free hand to her chest. Grant so envied that hand of hers. Then, and as if needing to calm herself, she took several deep breaths that enticingly lifted her full breasts…and all but sent Grant to his knees. What was he, to be acting this way, some hormonal junior high kid? But he was so distracted by her every movement that he had to think hard to catch up to her words. "You weren't standing there as long as I thought you were. Or you'd know that he's not mine."

Grant managed to nod. "Well. I guess I gave myself away." But he didn't care as a flood tide of relief washed over his heart. The baby wasn't hers. Not that it was any of his business. Not that he had any right to— *Oh, hell, Grant, get over it.* "Are you married?"

"No. Are you?"

"No." That exchange took about one nanosecond to complete. Then Grant stared at her staring at him. And in his mind's eye, he saw them again, back in college, all naked and tangled in his sheets, saw them all sweaty and— "So. Laura," he said desperately, his throat all but closing. When had it gotten so damned hot in here? "We're back to square one. Where *did* you get him?"

She blinked. "Who?"

And then it was funny. Thankfully funny. She *was* just as undone as he was. Good. He chuckled and pointed to the child riding her hip. "The baby, silly. Where'd you get the baby?"

"Oh. Him." She shrugged, sending her straight, strawberry-blond, blunt-cut hair cascading over her shoulders. "That is today's sixty-four-thousand-dollar question. Apparently, he just dropped out of the sky."

"Wow. Good catch," Grant teased. "I mean, what are we…about fifteen floors up?"

A bubble of laughter slipped past Laura's obvious attempts to squelch her humor. "Ha, ha. It won't be so funny when you realize that you're partially liable for him."

She was right. He didn't think it was funny. Grant cooled, right along with the room. He straightened. "Me? How?"

"Because he was left here sometime today in all the madness with *your* photo shoot. And now he's an abandoned baby. On *your* time."

"Ouch. Not good."

"No. Not good at all. But beyond that, I have no idea what to do here. And everyone seems to think I should automatically know because I'm female."

"Nice of them to notice, huh?" he said, as he raked his appreciative gaze up and down her shapely length. Anyone who wasn't very well aware of that fact was either blind or dead. Or both. But the baby… Hmm, perhaps he *had* dropped out of the sky. Maybe to help Grant earn a second chance with Laura, something he just now realized he really wanted. Not that he'd orchestrated this. But she'd said it herself—he was as liable for the baby's welfare as she was. His shoot, her firm. The two of them. Together.

Okay, two birds with one stone—take care of the munchkin until he was reunited with his parents, and at the same time use this opportunity to get close to Laura. It might not work, but he certainly had nothing to lose in trying, did he? The more he thought about it, wasn't Cupid portrayed as a little boy in diapers? And who was he to thumb his nose at a heaven-sent opportunity? The room began to warm again.

Laura nodded distractedly, bringing him back to the moment. "You never did say what you want here."

Now he laughed at himself. "That's another sixty-four-thousand-dollar question. One my father would like for me to answer. And quickly."

With her free hand, Laura waved away his answer. "I didn't mean in the larger Maguire bazillion-dollar sense. I meant right now. What do *you* want?" She hefted the baby on her hip, pointing to the little guy. "I don't mean to be rude, but as you can see, I'm a little busy right now."

"I do see. But I just stopped by to—well, it doesn't matter." *I just stopped by hoping to see you because I can't help myself.* How do you say that after ten years? Ten years after you walked out? Grant poked his hands into his overcoat pockets and focused on the dark pool adorning her skirt. "You might want to change him."

Completely deadpan, she drawled, "I wish to God I knew with what. You have any ideas?"

Grant grinned, pointing to himself. "You're asking *me* for help? After avoiding me for a whole month? You must be desperate."

She nodded, grimacing. "Pretend I am. And I haven't

been avoiding you. But you're here now. So what would you suggest?''

Grant grinned. *Well, well, well. Let the games begin.* ''Something dry?''

Laura's eyebrows slowly raised. ''You think?''

Vintage Laura. God, how he'd missed that. Grant chuckled as he shrugged out of his overcoat, tossed it over a chair and then…stood there, looking around the cluttered office. Mostly he hoped to spot a fully accessorized nanny, one who might be lurking in a corner and would step forward to rescue all three of them. But when one stubbornly didn't, he finally settled his gaze on Laura. ''All I've got is a handkerchief. It's big and clean, if not absorbent. It might work for a while.''

''A handkerchief? That's it?''

''Yeah. That and a safety pin, maybe. Or paper clips.''

Finally, Laura got on board. ''Hey, good idea,'' she blurted, brightening, much to Grant's delight, as she awkwardly tugged the baby up and out in front of her…at arm's length. Which apparently tickled the soaked little munchkin pink, judging by his outburst of chortling laughter. Laura looked past him to Grant and said, ''I'll hold him here. You look around for anything we can use. And hurry.''

''Sounds like we're in a gangster movie. 'I'll hold him here, Bugsy. You look around for da goods,''' Grant mimicked, garnering for himself a will-you-hurry-it-up tsking sound from her. ''All right, all right. Where's your sense of humor?''

''It fled with the wetness on my skirt, *Bugsy.* Just find something, please.''

''Yes, ma'am.'' With that, Grant hurried around the room, opening drawers, sorting through contents, pushing aside papers, closing drawers, picking up the various tools of an art director's trade, eyeing them for suitability and generally coming up empty-handed. Finally, he had to turn to Laura and ask, "What am I looking for, again?"

"Darn it, Grant." She stalked over to him, thrusting the kid into his Armani-suited arms. "Here. See how you like being Mr. Potty Chair. I'll look for the…stuff. You take his clothes off him before he gets a rash or something."

"Whoa." Grant held the sopping baby in front of him much like Laura had. The curly-haired waif eyed him with a disconcerting blue-eyed solemnity that sobered Grant. He said, "Hi, there. How ya doing, champ?"

The baby immediately gave him the Bronx cheer—a wet and resounding round of the raspberries. Startled, Grant looked past the kid to Laura, in time to see her handling the single biggest safety pin on the face of the Earth. "I don't think he likes me," he said.

Her attention riveted on the workings of the pin, Laura mumbled, "Yeah, well, I have my own problems with him. He thinks I'm his mother. That shows you what kind of a day we've both had."

Grant raised an eyebrow at the thought of Laura being a mother and considered her slender profile. A renewed awareness of her body's soft lines, her inviting femininity, so effectively hidden under her power-suit armor, assailed him. It was true. She was such a woman. She'd make a great mother. Suddenly realizing his own libido-warmed thoughts, Grant blinked. *Don't get carried away here. Go slow. Stick to the second-chance scenario, okay? Just remember what happens tomorrow.*

Tomorrow. That did it. More than a little disconcerted, Grant sought neutral ground by shifting his attention to the baby. And got a big surprise. The little boy appeared to be—Grant would swear it—assessing him. As if he were waiting on Grant to catch a punch line. Not able to stop himself, Grant asked the tyke, "What?"

But the chubby child blinked his baby blues, and the look was gone, leaving Grant sure he'd imagined that adult awareness in the kid's eyes. Surely he had. Surely.

"Okay," Laura cheered, pulling Grant's attention to her. He watched her walking toward him, her delicate-boned movements all fluid grace. But he immediately got over it when his gaze lit on the way she brandished the pointy end of the giant safety pin.

He gave a low whistle, telling the baby, "I'm glad it's you and not me she's coming at with that thing. Here. Look for yourself." As if the baby could understand, Grant turned him to face Laura. "See?" He shifted the boy's wide-eyed attention back to himself. "Yeah, I know. Listen, pal, unless she's changed a lot in the last ten years, you're in very real danger here. So my advice to you—and it's totally free—is…call your doctor. And your lawyer."

"THAT'S REAL FUNNY, Grant," Laura snapped at the ex-love of her life as she tried—again—not to laugh at him. Wasn't it enough that he exuded sexuality like a cologne? Did he have to be so fun and cooperative, too? Darn it, he'd always gotten around her defenses by being so sensible and by making her laugh. Well, not this time. Instead, she busied herself with gathering up all the clutter from Michelle's tilted drafting table.

With her urge to chuckle at Grant and thereby warm

up to him firmly under control, she directed him, with a pointing gesture, to lay the baby atop the cleared space. Not able to leave well enough alone, she remarked, "And you're just saying that, about doctors and lawyers, because my mother told you I'm not good with kids."

"Not good with them?" Grant placed the baby vertically on the table. The tilted table. "That's like saying Godzilla's just a big lizard. I think her exact words were— Oops!"

Laura screeched and Grant grabbed for Tucker as he slid into a wet heap at the bottom of the table. Plucking the stiff-limbed baby from the brink of disaster, Grant repeated, "I think her exact words were—" He lay the boy horizontally, only to have him again slide. "Dammit!"

"So far, Grant," Laura drawled, loving the hard time he was having, "you have my mother saying oops and dammit when talking about *me* as a mother. While it does sound like her—"

"*Meanwhile,* Laura, back at the ranch," Grant interrupted, his eyebrows veeing down over his straight patrician nose, "we need to focus. We're about to kill this kid. I'll put him on the carpet, and you can change him there."

"Me? As if. *You're* changing him."

"No, I'm not. You are. You're the female, remember."

Laura brandished the mother of all safety pins at him. "All right, that's it. That's three times in less than thirty minutes someone has felt the need to point that out to me. But nice try. And no, I'm not."

Grinning, Grant raised an eyebrow. "You're not what? A woman? I think I know differently."

Heat burst upon Laura's cheeks. She found she had to look down a moment before meeting his teasing expression. "I meant I'm not going to change him. You are."

Grant's eyes widened. "No, I'm not. He's not my baby."

"Or mine."

"Well, you found him. I'm not—"

"Wait a minute," Laura ordered. "Do you hear us, Grant? Do you? We're intelligent Ivy Leaguers with university degrees coming out the ying-yang. We run entire companies. And yet we can't even work together to dry one wet baby bottom. What is wrong with us?"

Grant quirked his mouth, looking so very handsome and boyish as he winked at the frowning baby he held. Then he turned to Laura and said, "I believe your mother said it best. Astonishing ineptitude. Genes didn't imprint parenthood. Vivian used phrases like that ten years ago when she tried to talk us out of getting married."

And why did we listen to her? Laura thought. "Imagine my mother counseling anyone not to marry. Mrs. Five Times Down the Aisle." Then a sudden shyness—all this talk about marriage, she guessed—overtook Laura, surprising her and again warming her cheeks. She couldn't remember the last time she'd blushed this much. Exasperated, she forced herself to don her "all-business" demeanor and said, "So...you want to try again? Use a little teamwork? I mean, you make baby products, and I advertise them for you. Surely we can figure this out."

Grant's tawny eyes warmed. He smiled, first at her and then at the still dangling, incredibly good-natured baby. "Sure," he told the little boy, then looked to

Laura as if to get her second. "Once more with feeling?"

Laura nodded, certain on some level that she was agreeing to much more than a diaper change. "Once more with feeling," she murmured.

From there, it got easy, if you don't count a mad dash for dry paper towels…another mad dash for more paper towels…safety-pin-poked fingers…an unfortunate geyser incident that had Tucker chortling at his own tinkling antics…a crawling chase after the bare-bottomed, scooting-away baby…and two totally unsuited-to-the-task adults, who were left sweaty and undone at the end of their ordeal. And with one baby wearing an expensive, monogrammed handkerchief—tissue-paper-stuffed for added absorbency—and secured with a sideshow-size safety pin. But…whew! Mission accomplished.

With a satisfied exhalation, Laura sat on her haunches. Grant followed suit. Hands to their respective knees, they stared at the blue-eyed baby lying on his back in front of them…and staring back at them. "So," Laura said. "What do you think he's thinking?"

"Well," Grant countered, "probably that he wishes someone on another floor—someone with a box of disposable diapers in their desk drawer—would've caught him when he fell from the sky." Then he looked at her and asked, "What do we do now?"

We. Laura liked the sound of that. She always had, when Grant was the he in the we. Getting back to the task at hand, she said, "Well, given the wet state of his clothes and the cold outside, we need to…" She thought. Then it came to her. "We need to rinse his outfit in the washroom sink and dry it with that air-blower thingie. I'm going to do the same for this spot on my skirt. And then I guess I need to—"

"There's no I to it. It's we," Grant countered. "*We* need to. I'm in this with you, Laura. Remember the liability thing?"

The warm "we" fuzzy that was spreading through her heart fizzled out on the word "liability." He was helping her for legal reasons. Of course. It made sense. But still, Laura felt the need to give him an out. She searched his face, looking for sincerity. "Are you sure, Grant? I didn't really mean that. You don't have to do this. He's not your problem."

"Sure he is. He's a baby. You had a baby shoot today with my company's name on it. And now you have a problem baby. So, it's my problem, too. End of story. Now, tell me what it is that *we're* doing, once you two are dry?"

Laura chuckled, hating that she was beginning to like him so much. Again. "Okay. I was thinking *we* need to take him to the police and file some kind of report. Or turn him over to them. Something like that."

Grant pulled back and stared at her, then extended his hand to shake hers. "Laura Sloan, you are brilliant."

Laura slipped her hand into his, feeling the strength and the warmth of his touch—so electric and yet so comforting—as his long fingers closed over hers. She'd almost forgotten how good he felt. How good he made her feel. But she masked her reaction with a light laugh and said, "Grant Maguire, I do thank you. But can you put that part about me being brilliant into our business contract?"

Still smiling—a teasing one, to be sure—Grant said, "Not on your life. Brilliant equates to more money. And the Tucker Company can barely afford you as it is. I can just see them telling me we have to give you up." Then his eyes grew heated. His voice dropped to a husky, intimate drawl. "I'd hate to have to buy the whole damned company just to keep you on. And I would, too. Because I'm not willing to run the risk of losing you...again."

Feeling very warm, almost liquid, Laura gulped and said, "You're not?"

"No," Grant quipped. "In the ad business, you're the best there is. Everyone knows that."

TWO TWILIGHT HOURS later, holding Tucker against her body, not at all sure where her arms needed to be to best support his sleeping weight, Laura cuddled the baby under her full-length, camel-colored winter coat. And hoped she wasn't smothering the kid. Or that she'd move her arm and he'd slide out from under her coat, hit the pavement, and she'd get stoned to death for child abuse.

As it was, only a tuft of his black baby curls gave him away to the casual passerby as Laura stood on the cold, wind-swirling, people-swarming street in front of the local police precinct. At her side, Grant clutched the baby carrier in one hand and worked on hailing a cab.

More than a few curious souls stared their way. The braver, nosier ones stopped momentarily. And Laura knew why. Even in celebrity-congested New York City, they wondered was this really Grant Maguire. Could it be, their excited stares seemed to ask. Yes. It could. It was. And she was with him. And drawing a lot of attention that she didn't want. Nor did Grant, she suspected. Especially since they had a baby nestled between them. She could already see those cozy Former Lover, Secret Baby headlines. All they needed to make this a full-blown disaster was for the paparazzi to show up—

"So, who knew the police wouldn't be able to help right away, huh?" Grant said, interrupting Laura's dread-filled thoughts. "'We'll take your information and have an officer call you later.' That's what they said?"

Laura nodded. "Yes. I have to admit, I never saw that one coming. Just like I never expected to see you hailing a cab."

Grant grinned. "Expected a waiting limo, did you?"

Despite the cold biting at her cheeks, Laura felt them heat up. "Well, yes. I could see why you wouldn't want one in college. But I guess I supposed that as you…got older, you'd—"

"Give in to my father's demands that I act like a Maguire?" The twinkle in his eye told Laura he was still giving the elder Maguire fits. And she liked him all the more for it. Then Grant added, "Not me. Limos are not my style. Damned things draw too much attention my way from every camera-carrying, money-hungry photographer out there. I'm worth five thousand dollars a picture, the last I heard. Makes me feel like there's a bounty on my head. Who needs it? Hell, I prefer being the average Joe on the street."

But you're not. And you never will be. Poor Grant. He'd always hated his built-in notoriety. In spite of it, he'd managed to make it on his own, avoid letting his father or his money control his life. And Laura respected him for that. But had he really had to abandon her to achieve independence? She just wished he'd allowed her to—

"Well, damn the police and their double homicide and bomb threats, anyway," Grant groused. "We have an abandoned baby here. And frantic parents out there somewhere. What's more important than that? Taxi!"

Laura glanced at the sleeping little boy whose apple cheek rested against her bosom. "Do you really think they're frantic, Grant?"

Laura looked up to see Grant lowering his arm and staring at her. "What do you mean? Sure they are. Wouldn't you be?"

"Well, of course I would," Laura protested as a very unexpected wave of protectiveness washed over her. Her arms tightened around the little tyke she held. "He's precious. And so helpless. I'm just hoping, for his sake, that there's a simple answer to all this, Grant. A mix-up of some sort. Like his mom thinks his dad has him. And he thinks she does. Something like that. You read about that all the time."

Grant smiled at her and gave her arm a reassuring squeeze that warmed her all the way through. "Yes, you do. And I'm sure that's it. Something simple."

Laura nodded, returning her attention to the trusting bundle in her arms. Okay, she didn't really believe the scenario she'd just offered. Where was the baby's coat? His food? A warm blanket? Proof that someone cared about this tiny stranger she'd dubbed Tucker. And what *was* his real name? Wouldn't his parents have met up by now and realized their mistake? Wouldn't they have called her firm? Or the police? But nobody in the whole of New York City seemed to be missing him. Nobody.

"You don't look convinced, Laura."

A bit startled—had he been watching her?—Laura shifted her gaze to Grant's handsome face. A frown deepened the lines on either side of his generous mouth. "I'm not," she admitted. "Are you?"

His frown became a slow smile, one at his own expense. "No. Hell, his parents may not even be on this continent, as we speak. They could be jet setting around the world, leaving him with his nanny. And the nanny could have dumped him when her boyfriend left for California. Who knows?''

Laura stared at Grant, recognizing the scenario he offered as similar to his childhood. The wealthy, absent parents. A succession of nannies. She'd always wondered if he knew how lonely he sounded when he spoke of his upbringing. What a poor little rich boy he'd been. And here he was, still defending his parents' lack of attention to him. Her heart suddenly lurching for him, Laura conceded, ''You're probably right. There could be any number of explanations.''

''Yes, there could be,'' Grant said, sounding stubborn. ''But you know, Laura, not one of them is good enough. We're talking about a baby here. You know he wants his mother. What kind of a woman would abandon her own child?''

''Excuse me?'' Laura retorted. ''His mother?'' Her face pruning with some unexpected, unacknowledged, long-denied, much-suppressed mothering feminist instinct, Laura snapped, ''Can we talk about his father? Where's the dad? Is he at some bar or sitting in front of a TV somewhere?''

''Well, how would I know? And do you hear yourself, Laura? You're judging people you don't even know.''

''I am? What about you, Grant Maguire? You said—''

''Shh.'' Grant gripped her arm firmly. Looking around, he whispered, ''I know what I said. But cool it with my name, okay? We're drawing a crowd here. Can the sleazy tabloid photographers be far behind? How would you like to be front-page news?''

Laura jerked her attention to her sidewalk companions. Sure enough, a crowd. A very interested crowd. With cameras. Oops. Turning her back to the bystanders and leaning into Grant, she said under her breath, "Fine. But I get to be mad about this. Not you. *You're* not the one who went from here to maternity in the space of an afternoon. I am. I'm the one who went to work this morning feeling like Murphy Brown and came out June Cleaver. Not you. See this?" She hefted the sleeping child. "I'm the one left holding the evidence."

Grant sobered, his expression as hard as his whispered words. "And where have I been, Laura? Right here at your side. That's where. Every step of the way."

Her long-repressed anger chose that moment to bubble over. "Well, how long do you suppose that will last…*this* time?"

Grant stiffened. "About as long as you'll last being a mother, would be my guess. Don't worry. You only have to do it for a couple hours. Until the police get hold of a caseworker or someone like that. Then this little boy will be off your hands. And you won't have to care about anybody."

With that, Grant went back to hailing a cab. He muttered something under his breath only a part of which Laura caught— *I don't know what I was thinking earlier*—before he blurted, "What the hell's the problem here? Are there no taxis left in this city?"

Laura stood there blinking, chilled and yet burning. Could she have sounded like a bigger wretch? Heck, could she have chosen a more public place for her bout of nastiness? Could her outburst have drawn more grinning, whispering attention their way? She glanced at Tucker. And felt even worse. He was vulnerable. Innocent. And so alone…like Grant had been all his childhood. And then it dawned on her—Grant saw himself in this baby.

Laura slumped, wanting to kick her own behind all around the city block while calling herself names, every one of which she felt she deserved. Feeling this way and even knowing Grant had as much to apologize for as she did, she huffed out her breath, told herself someone had to be the adult here and went about setting things to rights. "Gra—I mean...hey, you?"

He lowered his arm and turned to her, waiting. It was there in his eyes. The censure. The hurt. And, yes...the realized guilt. After all, he *was* the one who'd walked out on her all those years ago. She'd only spoken a truth. But probably one that didn't need to be said. At least, not in the way she'd said it.

"I'm sorry," she blurted. "I didn't mean it like that, what I said about you. Or the baby. Like I can't wait to hand him over to the first passing person willing to take him off my hands. It's just that I never thought I'd—I mean, I don't—"

"Laura," Grant cut in. "It's okay. You don't have to explain anything to me. This...the baby, me...we're pretty big shocks. I know that. And I'm sorry for reacting like I did. It's just that this little guy, I don't know, touched some chord inside me."

Laura's whole demeanor softened. "I know. I just...well, I just want you to know that I'm not mad at him. At the baby. I have nothing but sympathy for him. No, I'm mad at whoever dumped him. I mean, I may not personally want to get married and have children, but—"

"You don't?" Grant's voice held surprise. "You've decided that? You mean ever?"

Laura frowned. Somehow, her words and the decision

behind them when said aloud to Grant Maguire sounded as empty as her stomach was right now. But out loud she assured him, "I do. I mean forever. I decided that on the day you— Well, years ago. But it doesn't mean I'm not sensitive to children, that I don't have feelings for an abandoned one."

Grant's frown became a quick smile. "No one ever said you didn't. But forever is a long time." He turned away and waved down a cab, which began slowing in front of them just as camera-armed men and women began the flashing and popping that heralded the arrival of the paparazzi.

Blinking, turning away, huddling into Grant, Laura felt her face heat with thoughts of where these shots would turn up. And the questions they would generate. Just then, Tucker sighed in his baby sleep and rooted his little face against her bosom. Which caused Laura to lose all contact with her sanity and her hair to stand on end. "Grant? We need food. Now."

Grant stopped in the act of reaching for the cab's back-door handle to turn to her, frowning as the cameras flashed in his face. "Food? Laura, can we please discuss this inside the cab?"

"Oh, you bet we can. Look at him. Look what he's doing."

Grant stared at the rooting baby. His eyebrows slowly rose. "Well, I have to admire his taste...so to speak."

"That is not helping," came Laura's singsong response through gritted teeth.

Grant chuckled. "Okay, Plan B." With that, he opened the door of the cab and assisted Laura and her bundle in. He followed her, closed the door and scooted next to her, an arm along the seat back, all but around her as he huddled over her as if trying to protect her from the cameras' public eyes. Then he called to the burly, attentive driver, "Get us out of here. Just drive."

"You got it, mister," the man said. The cab took off with a squealing of tires that left the paparazzi yelling and chasing after them.

Once they were safely away, Grant leaned forward to tap the baseball-cap-wearing driver, "Take us to—" Grant's expression blanked. He turned to Laura. "Where do you live?"

Laura froze in her inept settling of the suddenly cranky Tucker to meet Grant's questioning gaze. "*That's* Plan B? My place was Plan A. But Plan B is now Plan A, and it needs to involve baby food. Seriously."

Grant frowned, looked confused and admitted as much. "I'm lost."

"Join the club, mister," the cabbie said. "Where we headed?"

Laura huffed out her breath, then gave their driver her address. *Men.*

"You got it, lady," he said. "All you had to do was say so."

Laura turned to Grant, hating the sudden tears that swamped her vision and blurred his face. If it weren't for Grant's warm and reassuring presence next to her, she'd lose it. Grant seemed to sense that. His demeanor softened as he squeezed her arm. "Hey, you. It'll be okay. I swear. We'll get you home and then I'll go get the baby something to…eat, I guess."

Heartened by his touch, by his seemingly earnest desire to help, Laura calmed down. "I appreciate everything you're doing, Grant. And I don't mean to act like such a shrew. I'm just…scared I'll do the wrong thing,

I guess. And he's so little. I'd just die if I hurt him or—''

"You're not going to hurt him, Laura. And as for the rest of it... Well, I owe you. We both know that."

Laura found it hard to hold his gaze. This was twice he'd said something about their past. But still, she heard herself forgiving him. "It's okay. That was a long time ago. We were both young and stupid. Bygones."

"No, it's not okay. I was wrong. And I'd like to make it up—"

A wailing, mysteriously muffled, cut off Grant's words. Then it registered, if not on the Richter scale, at least with Laura. *The baby. I forgot the baby.* With frantic fear streaking through her, she jerked her gaze downward and saw the baby as a disfiguring, coat-covered lump off to her side. Shrieking, she fished him out of the smothering folds feet-first and finally got him turned upright. Over the baby's screeches, she turned to Grant and yelled, "Dear God, I nearly—he's hungry, Grant. Do something."

"I know. I hear," Grant yelled. "But I have no idea what to get him. Or where. And you'd think I would, given my position at the Tucker Company, wouldn't you? But we don't do food. Just clothes. And I—"

"Hey! You two in the back seat?"

Grant and Laura turned to the cabbie, who managed to make himself heard over Tucker's continued wailing. "This is a very touching moment and all, Mr. Maguire—" Laura exchanged a look with Grant "—but maybe I could make a suggestion?"

"Is it anything helpful?" Grant yelled, his voice laced with New York savvy wariness.

Apparently unoffended, the cabbie shrugged and yelled, "Yeah. I got four kids of my own."

Grant gave Laura a bright thumbs-up and said, "In that case, sir, you are a godsend—and in for a big tip. Suggest away."

"I thought you'd never ask. Okay, we take you two home. Which, by the way, I shoulda known. Best part of town," their baby mentor yelled over his shoulder as he worked his cab through the choking, honking traffic.

"That was Plan A, remember?" Laura yelled as she patted the still-fussing Tucker's back. "That's where you came in."

The cabbie glanced in the rearview mirror. Laura met his black-eyed gaze as he said, "Excuse me. I wasn't finished. Hold him up, Mrs. Maguire. The baby, that is. Dandle him on your knee. They like that. They like to bounce."

Mrs. Maguire? Laura shot a look at Grant, who grinned and waved his hand, as if to say, *Let it pass.* All right. Fine. Then she mouthed, *Dandle?* Grant shrugged, his eyes wide and lost.

"Under his arms," the driver directed. "Hold him up. Let him balance on your knees and bounce himself. Otherwise, he's gonna be yelling his head off all the way home."

Wanting to avoid that nightmare at any cost, Laura did as she was directed. Sure enough, Tucker sobered, quieted and then, lo and behold, balanced and bounced and cooed and clapped his chubby little mitts together. Laura's shriek of happiness matched the baby's. "Look! He likes it!"

Wearing a sappy grin, Grant reached over her to allow Tucker to hold his finger and wave it around, too. "Hallelujah," he said.

"Yeah. I told you he would," their driver said, sounding like a smug old hand at this. Into the relative quiet, he continued outlining his plan. "Okay, now on the way to your place, there's a grocery with everything you need— Hey, shouldn't you two know this stuff by now? Your baby's got to be eight, nine months old. Oh, wait—you got nannies and maids that do that stuff, right?"

This was getting out of hand. "No, we don't. Because this baby's not ours," Laura offered, grinning desperately at Tucker, praying for his lightened mood to last. "We're not married. And we don't know whose baby this is."

The taxi veered to the curb and stopped. The cabbie turned to face them, suspicion written all over his pugnacious face. "Excuse me, lady?"

Laura suspected that she and Grant—and Tucker—looked like guilty children with their hands caught in a cookie jar. "No, it's okay," she rushed to assure him. "Remember you picked us up at the police station? They know all about the baby. We're keeping him for now. Until a report is filed and his parents can be found."

The man continued to stare at them. Individually. First Laura. And then Grant. And then Tucker. And finally Laura again. "Really," she felt compelled to add. "Seriously. It's okay. We're legitimate." It wasn't working. So she added, "Remember the crowd? All those cameras? That's because he's Grant Maguire. Just like you said earlier." Then she turned to Grant. "Show him."

"Show him *what,* Laura?" Grant asked pointedly.

But the cabbie raised a stop-right-there hand and assured them, "This ain't that kinda cab. So, okay, you're Grant Maguire. And she ain't Mrs. Maguire. And this ain't your baby. But it's all legit. Whadda I care? All I do is give rides to people who want to get from point A to point B.'' Having settled that, he went back to his plan. "So, on the way to the lady's place, we'll stop at this grocery—they're nice people. You should get to know them. And I'll go in with you and show you what you'll need to set yourselves up. How's that sound?''

"Like a twelve-course dinner featuring Chateaubriand and a two-hundred-year-old French wine," Grant quipped.

The cabbie raised an eyebrow at him, faced forward and muttered, just loud enough to be heard, "Yeah, that was probably what you two yuppies would-a fed the kid, too, without my help.''

And the scary thing was, Laura knew, he was probably right. Fearing for Tucker, fearing that she would innocently and ignorantly do something that would hurt the baby, like give him coffee in his bottle first thing in the morning—it was, after all, how she woke herself up—Laura stared into the little boy's chubby face, hoping, absurdly enough, for some sort of reassurance from him.

He winked at her.

3

NINE O'CLOCK. At night. Grocery store gone to, baby stuff picked up. Baby fed, but sloppily. Adults—Chinese take-out, delivered and eaten. No less sloppily. And now, like a lurking ogre, many dark and alone-with-the-baby hours lay between Laura and please-anybody-help-me daylight. Changed out of her Tucker-baptized suit into her pink and fleecy sweatpants, thick socks and a long T-shirt, standing next to Grant—who'd be leaving at any moment, she just knew it—Laura looked from her wristwatch to the child innocently sleeping in the pulled-out dresser drawer on the floor of her softly lit loft bedroom.

Sheet-wrapped sofa pillows crowded the deep drawer and cushioned Tucker's weight without folding around him. *Thank you for that tip, nice lady at the grocery store.* The baby's tiny fists rested to either side of his head. So far, so good. *Not.* Panic set in—but quiet panic, so as not to awaken the little boy. "Maybe this isn't such a good idea, Grant," Laura blurted softly. "Maybe you should take Tucker home with you."

Bent over, his hands resting on his knees as he aided Laura in her helpless staring at the sleeping baby, as if it were a duty assigned them both, Grant looked at her, frowning. He whispered, "Who's Tucker?"

"Him." Laura pointed to the baby.

Grant's eyebrows rose. Then a slow grin tugged at

his mouth as he looked from Laura to the baby and back to her. Still keeping his voice low, he said, "You're kidding. His name is Tucker? That's unbelievable. How'd you know?"

Laura let out her breath. "Well, obviously I didn't. And I still don't. His real name could be Edgar or Skippy, for all I know. So I just…call him that."

"You do?" Grant straightened, his expression still warm and amused as he put his hands on his waist. His rolled-up shirtsleeves exposed his well-developed, tanned forearms. The man must own a gym. "You named him Tucker? Like in Tucker the Bear? That's…I don't know, kind of sweet."

Laura felt suddenly too warm and too aware of their proximity. He was taking this all wrong. At least that's what she told herself as she tucked a stray lock of hair behind her ear. "Sweet had nothing to do with it. It just seemed like the obvious choice at the time. Especially since—and God only knows why or how—our proposed new Tucker the Bear logo is on the front of his sleeper."

Grant did a double take between her and the baby. "It is? I mean, I saw the bear, but I didn't realize—" Grant looked confused. "Now how did that—"

He took her elbow and pulled her down the three wide steps to the living room. Grant didn't stop until he'd positioned them in front of the bank of tall, narrow windows that replaced an east-facing wall and which blended with the moonlight to elongate their shadows across the hardwood floors.

Only then, with Laura's heart beating in time with her desire for him, with the way he looked in the moonlight, did Grant ask, "How *did* he get that logo on his sleeper, Laura? You haven't even shown *me* the design yet. In fact, that's why I came to your office today. To see it for myself, since it seems that you'd been avoiding me.''

Oh, she had him now. It was all she could do not to grin. He wasn't getting away with this one. Not bothering to extricate herself from his grip, since she really did like the proprietary feel of his hand on her, Laura cocked her head at a questioning angle. "You came over to see the design? Well, that meeting's scheduled for next Monday.''

He looked blank. Laura grinned, capturing her lower lip between her teeth. A gotcha moment. Grant didn't seem to want to look at her. Finally, he obliquely met her gaze and admitted, "I know that.''

"You knew? And yet you still came by? Why?'' *To see me? Please say to see me.*

Grant caved. "All right. You beat it out of me. I came by because...I wanted to see you. There. I said it. I wanted to see you. Happy?''

"Yeah,'' she blurted. "I mean...no. Okay, yes. I mean...you did? Why?'' Laura hated how girlishly excited her voice sounded, even to her own ears. And how her heart raced. Clearing her throat, forcing herself to speak normally, she added, "I mean, for business reasons? Or for, um, personal reasons?''

Grant frowned. "Personal reasons...that have to do with business. Family business.''

"Ah. Family.'' Silence followed. "Mine or yours?''

"Mine. I told my parents I'd seen you, that we're working together. And they...sent you their regards. Which I came by to convey.''

Not even her happy realization that he'd used the flimsiest of excuses to track her down could save Laura's expression, which soured at his mention of his parents. "Muriel and Stanton Maguire sent their regards? To me? No doubt, skewered on the end of a lance. So, Grant...how *are* your parents?" *Who hate my guts and always have. Me, the girl from the wrong side of the tracks. Not even close to blue-blooded enough for their only child and heir.*

"Older. Rethinking their lives. Things like that." Grinning, apparently unoffended, Grant crossed his arms over his muscled chest and stared at her, seeming to make it a point to look directly into her eyes. "But still as rich and snooty and condescending as ever." Laura's eyes widened. Enough to make Grant chuckle and add, "Surprised to hear me say that?"

She nodded slowly. "Yes, I am. Ten years ago I could have held your feet to the flames and you still wouldn't have admitted they were—" her courage failed her and she finished lamely "—all those things you said. Except the rich part. That was never arguable."

His chuckle turned to a bark of laughter. "That's true. But people—and I'm talking about me here—people change, Laura. They grow and mature." His expression warmed, as did his honey-brown eyes. "Meaning, I know and understand a lot of things now that I didn't before. So do they. To an extent."

Does that extent still end at a line drawn in front of me? she wanted to ask. But couldn't. Because after so many years, what was the point? "I'm glad to hear you—they—know and understand some things now. Good for you. All of you."

Another soft chuckle from him. "Yeah. Thanks."

"You're welcome," Laura responded, not really knowing what to make of Grant's behavior. Not only was he giving off intimacy vibes, but he acted as if she kept saying the wrong lines in a play they'd rehearsed. Clearly she wasn't behaving as he'd expected. Well, neither was he. Behaving, that is. Or maybe that was the problem. He *was* behaving, and she didn't want him to. *Get over him—it—Laura.*

But since he continued to stare quietly at her and to stir her feminine juices, Laura offered a smile, a tenuous one at best, one that didn't have a prayer of holding up under scrutiny. Sure enough, it slipped away the instant it formed. And left Laura feeling liquid and even more awkward than she had felt a moment ago. "Will you say something, please?" she blurted.

Grant spread his hands wide. "Sure. Like what?".

Exasperation—with him, with herself, with his effect on her—ruled. So she did the only thing she could. She attacked their past together. "Like saying how you should have believed me ten years ago when I told you your parents never missed a chance to remind me how you and I came from two different worlds. How I'd never fit in yours and you wouldn't be happy in mine. How they'd disinherit you if you married me. Things along that line. I think I deserve that much after ten years of silence. Call it closure."

"Closure." Grant exhaled and reached out to slip that same errant lock of hair behind her ear. At his touch, a betraying shiver of want, of need raced over Laura's skin. "All right. Yes, they said all that," Grant said, his husky voice seeming to make her vibrate where she stood. "I know it. And I'm sorry they acted like such jerks. But my parents weren't our real problem, Laura. Not in the long run."

"Oh?" she asked while managing to swallow the sudden thickening in her throat. "What was our real problem, then?"

"It's hard to say. I think we— Well, maybe *I* just wasn't mature enough to recognize and fight their social prejudices. Or maybe you and I just didn't love each other enough. Maybe that was our problem. I mean, we *did* let them pull us apart."

"Wow," Laura said quietly, blinking back tears. "I'm impressed. You've really given that some thought, haven't you?"

Grant smiled wistfully. "It sure sounds like it, doesn't it?"

"Yeah." Something, perhaps a seed of hope unacknowledged, died inside Laura. They hadn't loved each other enough, he said. Well, he certainly sounded over it to her. So what could she say? How could she answer that bit of closure? He'd left her no room to maneuver.

Grant turned from her to stare out the curtainless windows. "Just so you'll know...I blame myself, Laura. I was young and I was stupid. But I should have stuck by you. And told *them* to go to hell."

Laura's breath caught. She'd always wanted to hear him say those exact words. To acknowledge what he'd not believed before—his parents' treatment of her. And now? Well, he had. But she hated it. It seemed admissions of guilt were not what she wanted from him. And that surprised her. "You can't put all the blame on yourself, Grant. I mean, there we both were—the young and the stupid. We could've been a soap opera."

He chuckled but didn't say anything. Which left Laura staring at his broad-shouldered back and breathing in his male, citrus-cologned scent. And wondering about this new Grant who seemed so reflective and philosophic. What had happened to make him this way? Or—worse—could he be facing something now that had him looking at life differently? *And while we're at it,* she chastised herself, *what's wrong with you, Laura?*

Her first inclination was to deny the whole thing. But then, quirking her mouth into a grimace of guilt, she admitted that she'd been on Grant's case from the moment he'd stepped into her office this afternoon. When all he'd done was come to see her—as he had every work-related right to do—and then had pitched in to help her with the baby. And how had she, Ms. I'm Clinging to the Past, repaid him? By being snide and hateful. Darn it, she hated this vindictive side she had, just as much as she'd hated it in Muriel and Stanton Maguire. Those two and their, ''The rich are just different.'' *Boy, I'll say.*

What was even harder to take was that her mother agreed with them! It was after Grant had left her that she'd sworn off marriage. Nothing but chaos and hurt there. And nothing had happened in the interim to change her mind, despite two past-but-serious relationships. And despite that twinge of bridal envy she'd suffered earlier at the office.

Now, just hold on. Laura came to her own defense. *What single, thirty-year-old woman wouldn't suffer such a pang, wouldn't wonder about that walk down the aisle and who'd be at the end of it?*

Grant chose that moment to shake his head, chuckle and look at her. ''So, how is Vivian, anyway? I think I missed that outrageous woman almost as much as I did you. Talk about an Earth Mother. I thought she was going to feed me and pamper me to death.''

Grateful to him for the change in subject, Laura replied, ''You loved every minute of it. Admit it.''

''I do. I admit it,'' Grant said, in a more serious tone than Laura had anticipated. She sobered, stared at him, saw again the remnants of the lonely young man he'd been in college, the one who'd reached out to Laura's family and had been loved in return. "Vivian was more of a mother to me in the two years I was with you, Laura, than my own was back then. There. I said it. So give me my reward. Tell me my mother doesn't give a—"

"Grant?" Laura clutched his arm. "I didn't mean it like that. I know your mother loves you. And you love—"

His hand covered hers, and Laura swallowed the rest of her words.

He squeezed her hand. "I know. I'm sorry. It just…never mind." He coupled his apology with a crooked grin that grabbed her heart and begged her to let it go. "We were talking about Vivian. And you were trying to tell me how she is."

Self-consciously slipping her hand from his, Laura pushed her hair from her face and chuckled. "Well, you know my mother," she said slowly, making sure she sounded long-suffering. "She's as loony and generous as ever. And on husband number five. A nice guy named Irving."

Grant crossed his arms, striking a casual-conversation pose. "Yeah, I heard you say five earlier. And I'm sure he is. Nice, that is. Not named Irving. But, anyway, couldn't you warn this poor guy about your mother's tendency to collect men and use them for procreation?"

Laura shrugged, playing for drama with the next bit of information. "I would've, but—get this—it was already too late. She was pregnant—"

"Shut up!" Grant laughed, playfully nudging her shoulder.

Grinning, Laura raised her right hand. "Swear to

God. They had to get married. At their age. But I now have a great little six-year-old sister named Esther. You might be interested to know there are five of us kids now. Me, James, Cindy, Frederick and, like I said, Esther.''

"Wow. Five kids. Frederick and Esther I didn't know about. And just think, you haven't killed any of them yet. Imagine that.'' Laura smacked his arm. He chuckled. "But double wow for Vivian. Six years. That's a long time for her to stay with one man.''

"Isn't it, though? I'm hoping this one takes. But she still hears from Glen and Roger. And of course, they send her child-support checks.''

"Of course. Are they three and four? Do I know them?''

Frowning, she thought, and then said, "No, I don't think you do. Although keeping track of Mother's love life can be pretty confusing. No, wait—you did know Glen. But Roger was...well, after you. And poor old Ed—remember number two?—he died a while back.''

"Oh, man, I'm sorry to hear that. He was a hell of a poker player.''

"Yes. All those years with the vice squad taught him well. Too bad he was on the wrong side of that desk, huh? But finally,'' Laura added fatalistically, "there's *my* father.''

"Oh, no. Don't tell me that John—''

"Died? No, no. He's fine. Out in California. Joined a commune. He calls occasionally. Asks for money. I think he's trying to recoup all those years of child-support for me. But I send it, just to keep him out there.''

"Smart.'' Grant chuckled, then sobered as if he realized he'd laughed at her whole life. Which he had. "It's been tough, hasn't it, kiddo?"

Laura shrugged, warmed but yet self-conscious because of his obvious sympathy. "Tough? No. Colorful is more like it. And fun. Okay, wild and crazy. But I survived."

"You more than survived. You look great. You're doing great, too. I guess what I'm trying to say is...it's good to see you, Laura. Really."

Suddenly shy, Laura looked at her feet, wiggled her socks-encased toes, and finally looked at him. "Thanks. It's good to see you, too."

Grant's grin widened. "Uh-huh. That's why you avoided me for a whole month."

She straightened guiltily. "I did not."

"Did, too. But it doesn't matter now." He reached out and stroked her cheek. Laura's knees nearly buckled. It was only through incredible self-discipline that she managed to avoid closing her eyes and moaning at his effect on her. All these undercurrents were pulling her under...under his spell. Again. But when he said, "I've missed you," her willpower went up in smoke. Apparently, she'd needed those words from him.

Completely undone, but responding with a defensive fear that things were moving too fast, that she'd fall for him again with disastrous results, Laura resorted to humor. She forced a grin to her lips and said, "I'm glad you missed me. You deserve to, you rat."

But her words didn't have the lightening effect she'd expected. Grant nodded, as if agreeing that she was right, that he was a rat and that he did deserve to miss her. The quiet between them thickened. Slowly, Laura became aware of the moonlight, of how her shadow merged with Grant's and spilled across the floor. She became aware, too, of his proximity to her. Aware of her pulse-pounding reaction to him. Aware of how he was reaching for her. Of how she was melting into his arms and offering up her mouth—

Aware of how Tucker suddenly screamed at the top of his lungs, jarring every nerve ending Laura owned and jolting Grant away from her. Her heart thumping, her mouth suddenly dry, Laura was right on Grant's heels as he ran upstairs to the bedroom.

"What's wrong with him?" she cried as Grant leaned over the baby and lifted his rounded and drawn-up little body out of the drawer, holding him at arm's length and looking him up and down.

"I don't know, Laura," Grant answered, obviously agitated. "Maybe he just woke up to find himself in a drawer with a couple of giant strangers standing over him. Hell, *I'd* scream. Get that grocery-store lady on the phone. Maybe she'll know what we should do. Hurry."

Nodding, Laura went to grab the phone, only to stop in her tracks and yell, "I can't. I don't remember the name of the store. Oh, my God, what are we going to do, Grant?"

"Panic's good," Grant fussed, holding the child in front of him as if the baby were a live hand grenade with the pin already pulled. He tried making shushing and clucking noises.

Taking her cue from Grant, Laura helped out by making what she hoped were funny faces at the baby. The poor little guy. Like the forlorn and abandoned waif that he was, Tucker and his chubby-cheeked and squinting face steadily reddened. Real tears flowed from his eyes. Horrified, Laura clung to Grant's arm, admonishing, "Do something else besides making noises. They're not working."

Grant frowned. "Like those faces you were making worked? Here—" he transferred Tucker to Laura's arms "—you try. Maybe he wants his mother."

Even as she held Tucker to her heart and swayed, rocking him, anger flared through Laura. "I'm not his—"

The baby screamed even louder, pushing against Laura. Her eyes widened. "Take him. He hates me," she cried frantically as she juggled struggling baby limbs, trying desperately to maintain her hold on him. Or at least, her hold on a fistful of diapered bottom and one flailing arm.

Grant complied, swiftly drawing the screaming little boy into his arms. And then he did the same things Laura had...swaying and rocking, holding Tucker to his heart. Only this time, they worked. The baby instantly quieted. Again, Laura's eyes widened, this time with hurt. "It's true. He does hate—"

"Shh!" Grant warned, waving a hand at her from under the baby's bottom. "Don't wake him up. Look—" he pointed with the same hand, indicating the baby "—he's almost asleep."

Darned if Grant wasn't right. Tucker was almost asleep. So where did that leave her? The baby hated her. And loved Grant. Well, there you have it...the story of her life. Still, Laura forced herself to turn a you-did-it-he's-asleep smile on Grant. He winked at her and looked at the baby. Laura's gaze followed his. And then it hit her. Her expression softened. She swallowed, seeing the two of them through new eyes. Man and child. A father-and-son picture, commercial perfect. The handsome, virile male. Patting and rocking the perfect baby. Very touching.

Very pulse-pounding, actually. Satisfying. Nothing

moved a woman's heart more, according to all the industry research she'd read, than the sight of a man like Grant tamed, committed, paternal, the husband and father side of him on display. As she watched, she saw Tucker yawn, his round little mouth making the tiniest O Laura had ever seen. Her heart melted. Uh-oh. So it was true, all that industry research. Such a sight could make her fall in love. Fall in love? She was falling in love with him? Them. No. With Tucker. Or was it Grant?

Tucker drew up his chubby legs, which poked his unevenly diapered bottom out as he nestled closer to Grant. The baby murmured mama just before he clutched Grant's shirt in his fists and dropped off to sleep in earnest. Laura turned her wide-eyed stare to Grant and burst into quiet, shuddering tears. Grant's mouth dropped open as he gestured helplessly and mouthed, "What's wrong?" But Laura couldn't tell him. She shook her head and sobbed.

Which only seemed to make Grant more frantic. With his arms full of baby, he was forced to use body language expressive enough to earn him a place next to Marcel Marceau in the mime hall of fame. With only a frown, he asked her if she was in pain. At least, that's what she believed he was asking. She shook her head. Then he stiffened his arms, as if asking her if she wanted to take the baby. She waved him away, again shaking her head. He mouthed, "Why are you crying?" She shrugged and shook her head. She didn't know why.

Grant shrugged, then made a face, no doubt signaling his utter confusion as he looked to the exposed rafters of the high-ceilinged room. When he glanced at her again, his frowning expression begging for mercy,

Laura finally hiccupped and said, "The baby hates me. Will...will you stay with me—with us—tonight?"

THE NEXT MORNING, about eight o'clock, clad only in his boxers, after spending the night on the sofa bed, Grant rounded the corner from the dark and quiet living room and padded down the hall. Entering one of the two closed-off bedrooms on the other side of the kitchen, the ones he *couldn't* sleep in, Laura had protested, because what if the baby who hated her woke up, Grant shook his head. Sitting on the comforter-covered sleigh bed, he picked up the phone and dialed his home number.

Today being what it was in his life, he needed to check his answering machine. *Man, what a mess.* First Laura. Then the baby. And now today. Whoever was in charge of his life wasn't doing a very good job of scheduling the crises at reasonable intervals, he groused as he punched in the numbers and put the phone to his ear. He waited for the connection to go through so he could push the series of numbers and see if he had any—

"Hello?" A feminine voice at the other end—the other end being defined as Grant's place—said, "Is that you, son?"

Grant froze, momentarily startled. What was going on? "Mother?" Had he accidentally dialed their number in Chicago?

She sounded relieved. "Yes, it is. Hello."

"Hello, Mother." *Oh, man.* "Where are you?"

"Why, we're at your place, of course."

"Oh. I thought you weren't flying in until later today?"

"We weren't. But your father changed our plans. The weather, you know."

No, he didn't—it'd been fine last night. "Ah, the weather. So...when did you get in?"

"Last evening, late. It was a dreadful flight from home." *Dreadful? On your own private jet?* "Anyway, we came over this morning to your place. We used that key you gave us. And had to let ourselves in." She sounded aghast, as if she were sure there were people paid to do such things. "That horrid little doorman of yours—well, suffice it to say, he was of no help. And of course, we expected *you* to be here. Where are you? Wait. Your father wishes to speak with you."

Great. The parents were at his place. Grant ran a hand over his face and shook his head. *Son of a—*

"Grant? Is that you?"

"Hello, Dad. Yeah, it's me."

"Well, it's nice to hear your voice so early in the morning."

"Nice to hear your voice, too," Grant answered, even knowing that what his father really meant to say was, Where the hell are you.

Stanton Maguire confirmed his guess. "Where the hell are you?"

Grant would have chuckled, only it wasn't funny. "I don't work for you, Dad. You can't order me around. And not that it's any of your business, but I'm at Laura Sloan's. Yes. *That* Laura Sloan. *Why* am I here? Well, it's a long story. One I don't feel like going into right now."

A strained silence followed Grant's bluntness. In that silence, his jaw tightened. He was too damned old for this. He was thirty-two, for God's sake. And not subject to his father's approval—or disapproval—of his personal relationships. You'd think the old man would respect that. Or would at least concede it, since Grant was prepared to sign his independence away today—for his father's sake. And his health.

"Have you forgotten what today is, son?" the Magnificent Maguire, so dubbed by the tabloid journalists, suddenly asked, breaking the quiet between them.

"Hardly." He started to say more but his father asked him to hold on while he spoke with "your mother," as he called her. While he waited, Grant pictured his pending "coronation." There they'd all be…him, his father and his mother. And their pantheon of attorneys with the reams of paperwork to be signed. Paperwork that would give Grant the corporate reins to the vast Maguire holdings.

This event would mark the end of Grant's days of independence and the beginning of his father's freedom, of his retirement, forced though it was by his doctor's pronouncement that he either slow down or die. Which was why Grant had finally agreed to do this.

"This will be a great day, son," his father suddenly said into Grant's ear.

"I agree," Grant said automatically. But he wasn't focused so much on what his father was implying as he was on Laura. And on his rush to track her down before he did what he had to do—today. Timing had become everything. After today, his one-month association with the Tucker Company ended. And along with it, any chance to get to her. And he'd wanted that chance. Very much.

"You're awfully quiet, Grant. Having second thoughts?"

Grant mentally shook himself. "No, Dad. No second thoughts. I'm happy to do this." And he was, on one level. He loved his father. He wanted him to have a long life. To be happy.

"Have they found your replacement yet at the Tucker Company?"

"Yeah. A really competent, deserving woman. Deanna James. She'll do a great job."

"Good. Sorry to have to put you through this."

A sudden lump in Grant's throat took him by surprise. He'd never heard his father say he was sorry for anything. Or speak of his human vulnerabilities. "Hey, it's okay, Dad. Really. Your health comes first."

Stanton Maguire reverted to his customary gruffness. "Yes. Well. Don't miss this meeting today."

Grant chuckled. "I don't intend to, Dad. I'll be there. I know how important it is. I said I'd do it. And I will. I just—" The sound of running water came from the kitchen around the corner followed by a baby crying and desperate female shushing and cooing noises. Laura and Tucker.

Suddenly Grant felt like laughing. Could this be more insane? "Look, Dad, just…make yourselves at home and I'll— What? The Plaza Hotel? You're staying there?" *Hallelujah.* "All right. I'll meet up with you there. Eleven o'clock? Fine. No, don't send your car. I can— All right, see you then. Say goodbye to Mother—" The line went dead. Grant stared at the phone in his hand and finished, "For me."

Man, oh man. We're having fun now. Just like ten years ago. The circumstances might be different, but the choices were the same. Laura's needs or his parents' demands. *Great.* He usually liked to start his morning with some coffee, reading about life-and-death situations in the *New York Times.* Not living one himself, be it literal or figurative. Grant shook his head, pressed the ironically labeled End button on the phone, and glared at it as if it alone had flown his parents in early. What was he supposed to do now?

He couldn't leave Laura alone with the baby. She was scared to death and inept as hell with him. Just then a piercing baby scream rent the air. Grant stiffened. He could only hope she wasn't attempting to dry the child's bottom by putting him in the microwave oven, wet diaper and all. Then he instantly felt bad. Blame his fatalistic mood. She wouldn't do that. He suddenly straightened, staring blankly at the bowl-of-fruit painting hung on the wall across from him.

She might. He suddenly remembered Vivian telling him years ago about the time Laura had baby-sat for some new and unsuspecting neighbors. She had cleaned up their baby after a meal by hosing the kid down in the backyard, high chair and all. Grant jumped up and tore out of the room. "Laura?" he called as he rounded the corner into the kitchen. "What's—"

He jerked to a halt and stood looking around the darkened kitchen. The darkened, quiet kitchen. The darkened, quiet, devoid-of-humans kitchen. "Going on in here?" he finished. *Okay. Where are they?* Slowly he turned, scanning for some sign of life. *I know I heard them both yelling. I know I did.* Then he captured a familiar and blessed scent, along with gentle percolating sounds. His gaze lit on the Mr. Coffee. Yes. It was brewing the nectar of the gods. Relief washed over Grant. *I was right. She was in here. So where is she now?*

Confused, Grant shook his head.

"Grant? What's wrong? You look as if you've just seen a ghost."

Startled, Grant pivoted to face Laura—and saw her. *Everything I've ever wanted,* came his sudden, heart-stopping, ill-timed revelation. Yes, ill-timed. Maddeningly so. Why? Because his heart chose now to point out her everything-he-ever-wanted status to him. Today of all days. *Great.*

So there she stood, at the head of the three steps that led to her bedroom. All sleepy and warm, she held Tucker in her arms. Grant's eyebrows rose. For more than one reason. She'd never looked more desirable, for one thing. And for another, the little boy's head rested where Grant would like to find his own. Against her pajama-covered bosom.

What was all this coziness between these two after Tucker had shrieked the house down when she'd tried to hold him? After she'd sworn the baby hated her? And she'd cried and begged him to stay?

But anyway, here they were. And he couldn't deny his feelings. Didn't try to. How could he have known he was going to feel like this? Had he missed a meeting? Was he on the wrong page? Because here they were. The two people in all the world, he suddenly realized—and it nearly stopped his heart—that he wanted to love and to protect.

He did? Yes. The way he felt right now, the picture the three of them made here together, he knew he could dedicate his entire life to them. To keeping them safe and warm. To making them the reason he did anything and everything. And yet neither one of them was his. So what was going on here? Why was he feeling these things? He hadn't seen Laura in ten years. And the baby he'd known not much more than ten hours. He didn't get it.

"Are you all right?" Laura asked.

Grant blinked, focused, felt a little sick to his stomach. "Yeah," he assured her. "I think I am. I just—I heard you yelling earlier."

"Oh," she said, shrugging and nodding toward Tucker. "He yelled at me, so I yelled back at him." She smiled, a crooked smile that said, *I know it sounds stupid but it worked.* She looked at him questioningly. "Where were you just now?"

Grant jerked a thumb toward the bedroom. "On the phone. Answering machine. I was checking...." His voice trailed off. Couldn't he even finish a sentence? What was wrong with him? What was this fog surrounding him? Why was he hearing wedding vows as if they came to him through a mist? *To have and to hold...from this day forward...in sickness and in health...*

And if that wasn't strange enough, the baby—Grant became belatedly aware—was staring soberly at him, as if he, Tucker, was the one asking Grant to take the vows.

As Grant stared, drinking in the cozy scene before him and thinking of his life alone before yesterday, a life he swore to himself he couldn't go back to, not after this day, a cherubic smile lit Tucker's face. He raised his head from Laura's bosom and pointed a tiny, accusing finger at Grant. "Da-da."

4

IF YOU PUT boxer shorts on a Greek god statue, you'd have Grant in his early-morning attire, Laura thought yearningly. Unbelievable. The man may as well adorn a huge Times Square billboard. Not advertising anything. Just…adorn it. Because every woman in the world should be treated, at least once in her life, to the sight that greeted her now.

Laura finally forced her gaze away from Grant's impressive appearance to look into his surprise-widened eyes. Surprised by Tucker's calling him da-da, no doubt. Either that or he'd forgotten that morning did not become her the way it did him. Nevertheless, she grinned. "It hits you between the eyes, doesn't it? The first time he called me mama, I nearly fainted." She shifted Tucker on her hip and grinned at the clinging little monkey of a sweetheart. "Didn't I, precious?"

"Mama," Tucker dutifully repeated. Immediately Laura felt a warm wetness against her skin. Her mind went blank, and her mouth sagged open. What was it with this kid? Was he marking his territory? She tugged him off her sodden sweatpants-clad hip and held him out in front of her. "Yuck. I knew I should have changed you first." Laura's eyes widened. That didn't sound right.

She looked past the baby to Grant, who stood by the sofa bed. "Not that *I* need to be changed, mind you.

Well, I guess I do now. But I meant change him first as in before I came to see you—um, no, before I started the coffee. No, before I—''

''Laura? Just go change him, honey. I'll get you some coffee.''

Honey? The casual endearment floated along her nerves like butterfly wings. But had he heard himself? she wondered. She didn't think so, because he calmly turned and made his way toward the kitchen.... Laura watched him, waiting for realization to hit him. He skirted the— *Bam!* It hit him. He stopped dead, stiffening. And Laura, peering past the frowning little prune face of a baby that she held at arm's length, bit her bottom lip to keep from snickering out loud.

But all Grant did was clear his throat, shake himself and flex those gorgeous muscles of his, then continue to the free-standing breakfast bar, as nonchalant as you please. *The coward...*

Bzzzz. Laura jerked in the direction of the intercom and stared at the innocuous little box mounted next to the front doors. *No.*

She clutched the sopping baby protectively to her and stared at the doors. Then, immediately, desperately, her stomach sickening, her throat closing, she sought Grant. He'd come around the corner from the kitchen and stood as still as she was. His somber gaze rested on her and told its own story.

''Who could that be, this early in the morning?'' Laura asked, hearing and hating the wooden sound of her voice. She couldn't seem to look away from Grant's compelling eyes as she silently begged him to tell her this wasn't who she feared it was. Feared? Shouldn't she be glad? After all, wasn't she the one who didn't want babies, who swore she couldn't take care of one?

"I don't know who it could be," Grant answered in an equally flat tone. "You expecting anybody?"

"No. Are you?"

"No. No one knows I'm here. Well, except my parents."

Laura swallowed. "Your parents?"

"Yeah. They're at my place. It's a long story."

"Oh. Then it must be the authorities. For Tucker."

To Laura's eyes, Grant seemed to settle in place. "I think it is."

Tears sprang to her eyes. "I know it is," she said.

The buzzer sounded again. Grant looked in that direction and slowly swung his gaze to her. "We have to let them in."

"I know."

"You okay?"

"No." Laura shifted the clinging little boy's weight and cradled his warm, dark head to her bosom. Silently, the child clutched at her T-shirt with both dimpled little hands. And broke Laura's heart. Poor little guy. He knew he'd better hold on. She was liable to drop him at any moment. So maybe it was best they took him away now. Before she did something stupid, like lose him. Or lose her heart to him.

"You want me to answer it?" Grant's words captured Laura's attention. She saw him nod in the direction of the double doors.

His amber-colored eyes held her gaze, told her that he cared, that he was here for her. She needed that from him. Even as her heart swelled with ragged emotions, she realized that his whole demeanor implored her to be strong, to be adult and rational. But Laura felt none of those things. "I can't do this, Grant."

A strident, insistent double buzz of the intercom accompanied his answer. "You have to." Then he added in a softer voice, "It might not be them. It could be anyone."

Laura shook her head. "No. It's them. They've come to take Tucker away."

Grant slumped. "I know." He spoke rapidly. "This is crazy. He's not ours, Laura. How could we have gotten this attached to that little boy so quickly? It makes no sense."

Ours. We. "And yet?" she probed, hearing the undercurrent in his voice. He was as undone as she was. And that said so much about him, about the man he'd become, that he could put her emotions first, that he could feel this strongly for an abandoned baby. More than anything else he could have said or done, it was this aspect of him that had Laura falling in love with him again. If indeed she'd ever stopped loving him.

He stood there, staring at her, no doubt ordering his thoughts, coming to terms with the turmoil that rocked them both. "And yet," he finally said, "I'm wishing I were a superhero and we could fly out of here with him." He stared at her and straightened, his features hardening as if he'd come to some conclusion.

In the next instant, he strode purposefully for the doors. "Which tells us everything we need to know, doesn't it? One more day with Tucker and we'd be fugitives with someone else's child. And we don't even know what the hell to do with him. We've got him sleeping in a drawer, for crying out loud. The kid probably has a nice crib and loving parents somewhere. It's best they take him home now, Laura, so we don't get any more attached than we already are. We need to quit playing house, quit acting like we're a family and he's our child. It's nuts."

As harsh as his words were, Laura knew what he was doing. He was hardening his heart, convincing himself he could give up the child he'd obviously come to love. And the very fact that he had to harden his heart only melted hers. Again he was showing how much he cared. About her, that she'd be hurting. And about Tucker, an innocent little waif. She wondered if Grant knew how much more he'd revealed. About them playing house. About Tucker being theirs. Was this Grant's way of saying he wanted that to happen…with her?

And if so, was that what she wanted, too? Really wanted? Down deep inside, in her gut, in her heart? She needed to decide. But hadn't she already decided, she wondered as Grant stood there, giving her time, despite the buzzer's insistent ringing. Was that why she felt so attached to Tucker and why letting him go hurt so bad? Could it be that she feared losing Grant when Tucker was gone? Was she clinging to Tucker as a way to hold on to Grant, as crazy as that sounded?

With those questions unanswered, what else could she do? Grant was right. They were fooling themselves here. Tucker wasn't theirs. And they couldn't entangle him in what was yet to be explored between them. It was for the best, then, that the authorities were here for him.

Grant cut into her thoughts. "Laura? Are you ready?"

She blinked and saw Grant staring at her, his finger poised over the answer button. Waiting on her to end their unconscious charade. She couldn't speak. Her woman's heart was telling her to do the right thing by the baby. But it was also her woman's heart—a heart that was breaking—that had her unable to answer

Grant's question with anything but a nod. A final nod. An ending.

Laura shifted in place, feeling the baby's warm weight against her, smelling his acrid wetness that made her shirt cling to her side. And feeling her heart thump out its sad little beat. Then she realized that Grant still hadn't pushed the button. Again Laura nodded, this time adding, "Go ahead. Like you said, let's get it over with. He belongs with his real parents."

Grant stared at her, his heart in his eyes. "Laura, I—" he blurted, then stopped. Firming his lips together, he blinked and exhaled. "I hate this." Then he turned and pushed the call button, all but spitting out his words. "Yes?" he said into the speaker.

From where she stood, across the big and open room, up the three stairs, all Laura could hear was a metallic, garbled voice replying, a man's voice. But she didn't have to hear what he said to know who he was, what he wanted. Because she had Grant's expression to go by. And it told her plenty. It was the authorities. And they were here to take the baby away.

"THIS IS Officer Hawkins from the local precinct. Can you let me up, please?"

It was the hardest thing he'd ever done. "Sure," Grant said and depressed the button. Then he stared at the green doors, wanting only to turn to Laura, to convey in some way that he felt what she did, that he was here for her. *Yeah. Time permitting.* Grant clenched his hand into a fist. He wanted to hit something. How in the hell could he leave for a meeting after this guy came up and took the baby? Laura would be a mess. And he wouldn't be here to help her through. What the hell was he supposed to do?

Forget it. I'm going with my heart. Grant turned. "Laura, I—" But she wasn't there. Her or Tucker. Grant's stomach bottomed out. "Laura? Where are you?"

He listened, searching the room with his gaze. No answer. No movement. What was going on? It was all one big room at this end of the loft. He should be able to see her. She hadn't had time, even if she'd run, to get to the enclosed kitchen and bedrooms. Why would she do that, anyway? She was too intelligent to hide from the police. She knew she couldn't keep the baby. But still… "Laura?" he called, louder this time. Again nothing. Not a sound.

At the moment Grant realized he was standing there in nothing but his boxers, the doorbell behind him rang. Too late to scramble for clothes. *Just go with it. One clean cut, and it's over with.* Right. He opened the door, saw a lone, generic uniformed cop who nodded a greeting. Grant returned it, saying, "Hello. Come in."

"Thank you," the medium-size, unremarkable—except for a craggy face—policeman said as he nodded, stepped over the threshold and removed his hat. "Sorry to bother you so early, Mr. Sloan, but I figured with your baby missing and all, you probably didn't get too much sleep anyway."

In his emotional fog, and figuring that maybe he hadn't heard the policeman correctly, Grant frowned. "What? Who?"

"Officer Hawkins, sir. I was just saying I'm sorry for your problems."

"My problems?" Grant stared at him. What did this man know of his problems? But what could he say except, "Thanks."

"Yes, sir," the officer said. Obviously ill at ease, the

policeman added, "Normally, uniformed officers such as myself don't make these calls. But I just got off duty. And my desk sergeant called me on the radio and asked me, this being the kind of case it is, to stop by and tell you not to worry, that your report was forwarded to us early this a.m. We're on it, assigning the case. So if you can just hang on here, someone should be out later to take care of things."

What's this? Grant's swelling heart wanted to know as his brain absorbed the man's words. *This guy won't be taking Tucker? Someone else, someone later, will?* Good. A temporary reprieve. Sure, one that would only make it harder to give Tucker up later. But still, a reprieve. Time to put this in the proper perspective. Grant grinned. "Man, you don't know how glad I am to hear that. We've just been crazy with this."

The officer nodded, a sympathetic smile tugging at his lips. "Yes, sir. We thought you would be. Anyways, try not to worry. Even if you don't hear anything right off, that doesn't mean we're not working on it. It could even be a couple of days."

"Days?" Grant's momentary elation evaporated. In two days, they'd need a crowbar to get Tucker away from Laura. And from him. "That long?"

Officer Hawkins's expression sobered right along with Grant's. "I understand your impatience, sir. I'd feel the same way. But there's no way to predict these things. All I can say is everyone is doing their best to find your son."

Grant stared at the man. "My what?" What the hell was the man talking about? "I'm not sure I understand—"

"I know you don't, sir," the policeman cut in. "That's why it's best to leave these matters to us.

We've got it under control. So I won't keep you. I know you probably want to be with the missus—''

"The missus?"

"Yeah. Just try to think positively," Officer Hawkins continued. "Most of the time, cases like these work out well. It's usually someone who wants a baby of their own but can't have one. So they take good care of it. That doesn't make it okay, I know. But hey, it's something to cling to. So, don't worry, someone will be out later. If you hear anything first, though, call us. Other than that, we'll be in touch."

With that, the officer settled his hat on his head, nodded farewell and added with a smile and an attempt at humor, no doubt, "If you'll excuse me, I need to get going. The squad car's double-parked. I'd hate to get a ticket."

"I guess so," Grant said, still somewhat lost. As the uniformed cop walked out of the apartment, Grant said, "Thanks for coming by. So, I guess we'll just wait to hear from you?"

"That's a good plan, sir," Officer Hawkins said. Then he strode toward the elevator.

Grant closed the door and stood there, staring at it. What had just happened here?

"Grant?"

Startled by the sound of Laura's voice, Grant jerked around to see her behind him. She'd changed into jeans and a sweater and had the baby bundled in a big woolen scarf, ready to go. Held in Laura's arms—awkwardly, as if he were a watermelon—Tucker gripped a nursing bottle in both hands and ate his breakfast. Grant's gaze went to a woven grocery bag, lumpy with its contents, at Laura's feet.

Then he looked in her eyes, saw the strain there and

spoke softly. "Where'd you go? I turned around and you were gone. I even called out to you."

Her expression crumpled. "I know. I heard you. But I couldn't—he was wet. So I changed him…and then I changed myself," she said, pointing to the jeans she wore. "And he was hungry. So I gave him the bottle I fixed for him while you were on the phone. And then—" she nudged the bag at her feet "—I got all his stuff together, the stuff we bought him last night. The formula and bottles…baby food…diapers…little toys."

Grant watched her talk, heard her sniff and wanted to hold her, to kiss her, to save her this heartache. She looked so sad. But when she was done with her litany, he couldn't help offering a tender smile. "You've been busy."

She nodded, peering past him. "Who was it? Where are they?"

"It was a policeman. And he's gone."

"Gone?" Laura frowned. "Without Tucker?"

Grant chuckled. "Apparently. Since you're still holding him."

Her frown deepened. "You're telling me there was no caseworker with him?"

"I expected the same. But no, he was alone."

She blinked. "Well, was he here for Tucker?"

"Not exactly."

Laura's forehead creased. So did Tucker's. "Grant, what are you talking about? Spill the details, will you? Is the policeman coming back or not?"

"I am trying to tell you, Laura. He's not coming back. Not for a while. Maybe not even for a couple of days."

Laura's gray eyes widened. So did Tucker's blue ones. He popped the bottle out of his mouth and stared at Grant as Laura asked, "Days, Grant? *Days?* What happened here? What'd he say? No, wait—what did *you* do? Did you pull your Magnificent Maguire routine? You did, didn't you?"

Offended, Grant straightened, protesting. "I did no such thing. But had I—well, I would've been doing it for you. Because of how you feel for the baby."

The baby looked up adoringly at Laura and said, "Mama."

Laura poked the bottle into the baby's mouth. "No fair. Two against one." Then she leveled her steely gaze on Grant. "That proves it—your 'I did it for you.' That man came to get this baby and return him to his lawful parents, and you abused your Maguire influence. Admit it."

"I will not," Grant said stubbornly. Then he suddenly remembered to add, "Because I didn't do it. Hell, I didn't get three words in edgewise with that guy. He didn't even recognize me. In fact, he kept calling me Mr. Sloan."

"Mr. Sloan?"

"Yeah. And he was talking about my missing baby, and not—"

"Oh, my God," Laura blurted, her eyes wide with disbelief as she shifted the bottle-sucking baby to one arm and grabbed Grant's forearm. "They got the report wrong."

Her nails dug into his skin, but Grant didn't even flinch. "What?"

"They got it wrong, Grant. They obviously think *our*—mine and yours—our baby is missing. Remember the precinct? The phones ringing. Everyone coming and going. The noise. I knew that desk sergeant wasn't really listening to me. And he never even saw you and the baby, since you were standing off to the side. Remember how I told you he brushed me off, how he barely made a note of what I was saying? And let's face it, weren't you surprised that they didn't take Tucker right then?''

Grant's chest tightened, recognizing the truth of what she said. When Laura let go of his arm, Grant ran a hand over his face and stared at her. "Oh, man, you're right. That's why that Hawkins guy called me Mr. Sloan. You gave them *your* name and address. And I answer the door. Put two and two together—I'm Mr. Sloan.'' A chuckle of disbelief over this comedy of errors escaped Grant. "What are we going to do?''

"What are *we* going to do?'' Laura repeated. "*We're* going to take this baby down to the police station, hand him over, and straighten this whole mess out. Before the police figure it out first, and *we* get arrested.''

She sounded so logical. Grant hated it. "I thought you'd be happy for this reprieve, Laura. Ten minutes ago you couldn't stand the thought of turning Tucker over to the authorities. Why are you so determined now? Why the rush? Is the mothering thing not sitting well with you?''

Her eyes rounded to a helpless vulnerability. "That's a terrible thing to say, Grant. I… It's just the right thing to do,'' she said softly. "For Tucker.'' Her eyes suddenly swam in tears. "He's not ours—mine, I mean. If I don't do it now, I don't think I—''

"I'm sorry, Laura,'' Grant interrupted, feeling like a worm. "What a jackass I am to say such a thing.'' He reached out, squeezed her arm tenderly. "I shouldn't have said that. And I really don't mean it.''

Laura let out a shuddering sigh. And Grant wanted to die. He'd hurt her terribly in the one area she'd always been vulnerable—her aptitude as a mother. Or her lack thereof.

"It's okay. We're both upset." She pursed her lips and hardened her expression. Then, with a mischievous glint in her eye, she added, "But if you ever say that again, I'll kick your butt."

Grant's answering chuckle, rife with relieved humor, was cut off when Tucker chose that moment to show he'd been listening and what his opinion was. Out popped the bottle from his mouth. "Butt," he repeated, loud and clear, right into Grant's face.

Grant exchanged a shocked look with Laura. And then, over her laughter, he focused on the baby in her arms. "Hey, I said I was sorry. How about you cut me some slack, huh?"

Having made his point, Tucker raised a baby eyebrow and poked the bottle into his little mouth and occupied himself with the remainder of his breakfast. Which left Laura and Grant to sort out their lives. Laura was the first to start. "So, what do we do now? Do we take Tucker in to the authorities or not?"

Grant exhaled, shaking his head and running a hand through his hair. "No. I don't think so. Look how they messed up a simple report. What are they going to do with something as small as a baby down there? He could end up filed away as evidence, for crying out loud."

Laura nodded. "Yeah, well, he's not exactly safe here, either. So your vote is to keep him? For now, I mean."

Grant stared at her and finally accepted that he wanted that more than anything else in the world. "Yeah. That's my vote. We keep him until his real folks show up." It was genius. Inspired genius. "That's it,

Laura. We keep him and see if his folks come back. If they're good people and this was some crazy baby-sitting snafu or something, it would be easier if they didn't have to bother with the police, and—''

''Then we could just end it happily right there,'' Laura finished, her eyes bright. ''And give him back. I'll call right now, see if they left a message on my voice mail.'' Her expression fell. ''Oh, Grant, what if they're lowlifes? What do I do?''

''Then call the police and turn them over, too. Along with the baby.''

Along with the baby. Grant's words hung in the air between them. No matter which scenario played out, the result was, and always would be, that they'd have to give up Tucker. Suddenly, Grant couldn't look at Laura.

And she didn't seem to be able to make eye contact with him, either. ''Okay, here's something else,'' she finally said, sounding forced but practical. ''What about work?''

''What about it?''

''My day is full. As I'm sure yours is. So, who takes him in with them?''

Grant met her gaze. ''I hadn't thought about that.''

''Me, either. Until now. So, how do we decide?''

He shrugged. ''Paper scissors rock?''

She grimaced. ''Grant, that's childish.''

Grant stuck his fist out. ''No, it isn't. Come on. Loser takes the baby.''

Laura nodded the baby's way. ''He can hear you.''

Grant eyed the watching munchkin and grinned at him, winking. ''Sorry about that, buddy.'' He looked at Laura. ''Okay, the *winner* takes Tucker.''

She still didn't like it. It was there in her eyes. But she caved, setting Tucker on the floor with his bottle and sticking her fist out, holding it atop her other palm. "Oh, all right. Just do it fast before he crawls off and gets stuck under the sofa and a dust buffalo eats him."

Chuckling, Grant said, "Remember when we used to do this before?"

She almost met his gaze. But not quite. "Yes."

Grant stared at her, noting the curve of her jaw, the slender column of her neck, the lift of her breasts. "After sex," he murmured, seeing her face redden and feeling his own blood surging. But not to his face. "To decide who went out to get the greasy bacon cheeseburgers we always craved afterward?"

Her skin became candy-apple red, and she fidgeted in place. "I said yes, I remember. And I always lost and had to go. What's your point?"

"Look at me, Laura." She shook her head. He lifted her chin with his thumb and forefinger. Saw the raw desire in her eyes. His breath caught. He had to wet his suddenly dry lips. "Is that something you still do...the cheeseburgers, I mean...after sex?"

She blinked, her gray eyes warm but wary. Self-protective. "No, I don't. Apparently that was just something with you. Are we going to do this or not?"

Grinning, feeling as if he'd won some victory and wanting her so very badly, Grant got a hold on his libido and mimicked her pose. "Okay. On three. One. Two. Three." He splayed his fingers out flat. She kept hers in a fist. "Ha! I won. Paper wraps rock. Tucker goes with me." Then he heard himself. His expression fell. "Eww. I won. Tucker goes with me."

"No, he doesn't." Laura scooted away, grabbing the abandoned nursing bottle and Tucker as he pulled himself up to the coffee table and reached for a crystal candy dish. Holding the baby the way she would a football again, she jerked to face Grant. "He's going with me."

Grant cocked his head. What was going on here? "No, Laura. He's going with me. We just decided that." He walked over to her and held out his hands. "Seriously. I want to do this."

"No." She pivoted, keeping the baby away from Grant.

"Come on, Laura." Grant waggled his fingers. "You're going to make him dizzy. And his stomach is full."

Laura's eyes widened and she jerked her gaze to the grimacing baby. "Don't even think about it." She turned to Grant. "I ought to let you. You deserve it. And besides, I really can't take him with me. I won't even be in the office most of the day. I have to call on clients and—"

"So hand him over. I'm not the one arguing."

She jutted her chin out and kept her hold on the baby. "Did you know it's snowing?"

"Snowing?" Grant started for the windows to see for himself. "Oh, that's just what we need. I have an eleven o'clock meeting today that's vital."

Laura and Tucker, the latter still dangling off Laura's hip, her arm around his middle, were right beside him. "Like my appointments aren't?" she challenged.

"You don't understand," Grant said, staring out the window, watching the avalanche of big, fat, white, blinding flakes fall from bruised clouds. *What a mess.*

"Understand what?" Laura persisted.

Grant turned to her, holding his hands out for the baby. "Never mind. It's that whole long-story thing. With my parents. Hand him over."

"No. You probably can't even keep a houseplant alive."

"Hey," Grant protested. "I'm not totally stupid, you know. I'm getting ready to head up major corporations—"

"Uh-huh. Like that counts. Name one living human being you've ever cared for. I mean, taken care of."

Grant heard her first words, but ignored them. "All right. Me," was his answer. "I've taken care of me. And I'm obviously alive."

Laura's bottom lip poked out stubbornly. "That doesn't count."

"The hell it doesn't. Come on, Laura, I'm a grown man. You women aren't the only ones with nurturing instincts. I think I can look after one tiny baby. Even in a snowstorm."

"Oh?" Laura chirped, a danger signal Grant knew from way back when. "Can you? Then here." She plopped the startled baby and his bottle into Grant's arms. "Go ahead. Do it." With that, she jerked around and walked away. Suddenly she stopped, turned to face him and pointed to the woven grocery bag by the door. "There's his stuff. Have a nice day." She flounced off, stomping up the stairs to her bedroom and calling over her shoulder, "I'll let you know if his parents show up."

Grant watched her go, enjoying the view as her bottom bounced enticingly. Then he sighed. Oh, man, he'd gone too far. Grant glanced at the blue-eyed baby—the blue-eyed and ticked-off baby. Who pulled the empty plastic bottle from his little mouth, tossed it as far as he could, grabbed a handful of Grant's chest hairs...and yanked hard.

5

SHE COULDN'T do it. She couldn't stand one more minute of her workday wondering every single second how Tucker was, how Grant was, how Grant was doing with Tucker. And if she'd ever see them again. After all, she'd told Grant to take Tucker's stuff with him. And Grant certainly didn't have anything at her place to come back for. *Except me.* She sniffed. But why would he? *Selfish, hard-nosed brat. You deserve to be alone.*

Yeah, well, I am, okay? So leave me alone. Laura finally admitted that she'd succeeded in making a big fat mess of her workday, too. And it was only early afternoon. She stood at the window in her office, shivering, her arms crossed under her bosom as she watched New York City lose its battle with Mother Nature's vindictive fury. The storm of the century, they said on the radio.

Outside, it certainly looked the part. The blinding snow fell thick and heavy, like the main curtains at the Met after an opera's final act. The wind blew in bone-chilling swirls, bending defenseless trees and people to its will. The narrow streets, a congested nightmare even on the best of days, were treacherous, from what she could see of midtown Manhattan. Traffic was snarled, tangled, wrecked and all but at a standstill. And twice already the power had flickered off and back on. Not good.

Worse, all her meetings that day had been canceled. More than one of her clients had said they were shutting down early so their employees could get home. It was the only sensible thing to do. In fact, she figured she might as well do the same. Half the people hadn't been able to make it in, so nothing was getting done, anyway.

Normally such a scenario would make her happy. After all, this would be a midweek, weather-imposed holiday. She pictured her afternoon, trying to convince herself that being alone was what she wanted. So after she fought the battle outside and got home, she insisted, it would be great. She could put on her sweats and curl up with a good book. There. See? She smiled. That sounded great. That and a nice cup of cocoa. Just her, maybe some soft music and the sofa...

Still unmade. From where Grant had slept in it. Laura blinked, remembering the battle she'd fought with herself last night. She had tossed and turned, burning with his closeness to her, burning with the need to feel his hands on her body. And he hadn't helped any. She'd heard his restless movements and the squeak of the sofa as he'd gotten out of bed more than once. And she couldn't resist the temptation. Once again she could see herself squatted behind the railing, her presence cloaked in darkness, watching him staring out the windows. Dear God, the sight he'd made, bathed in moonlight. All warm muscle and male perfection.

So what had stopped her? She had a pretty good idea what Grant's reaction would have been had she gone downstairs to him. So why didn't she? Well, because of that drawer still sitting on the floor by her bed, mainly. And the baby in it. It hadn't seemed right— even with the myriad other reasons she shouldn't have aside—to give in to lust with a little innocent right there. How did married people do that? Have sex, she meant.

Sex. Grant. But it was about so much more than sex. It was about— *No, don't say it. Don't admit to that.* She squeezed her eyes shut, refusing to let the tears fall. *Just stop it. You had your chance. And you blew it. Now you don't know where he is. Where they are. Or if they'll even come back. And why should they? You walked away from both of them.*

Just as she was about to admit to herself why she felt like crying, the phone on her desk rang. Laura froze. *Grant!* She ran for the phone. Which had the audacity to be positioned at her desk's opposite end. All but falling into her rolling chair, with a wall at her back and the heavy wooden desk in front of her, Laura made a grab for it. And knocked it off her desk. It quit ringing. "Dammit," she shrieked. "Don't hang up. Hold on. I'm coming!"

And then, regardless of panty hose and decorum, she hiked her slim skirt to her hips and scrambled onto her desk, lying atop it on her stomach, with papers scattered everywhere, and pulled on the cord until she fished the receiver up to her ear. "Grant? Is that you? Is the baby okay? Where are you? I'm sorry. I don't know why I—"

"Laura? Is that you, honey? What's wrong? I *knew* something was wrong. Irving? Come here. I told you I know when something's wrong with one of my babies. I am, too, psychic. You talk to her. She'll tell you I am."

This was not happening. It was her mother. Calling from Rhode Island. *Please, God, let her be calling from Newport.* Laura slumped like a dead weight across her desk, but managed to keep her hold on the receiver.

"Mom? Hello? You don't need Irving to— Hello, Irving. No, I'm fine. Yes, she's psychic. Just go with it, Irving. It's easier. You've had six years to get used to— What? It's snowing there?" *Whew. They're at home.* "Yes, it's snowing here, too. What? Why do you want to know that?"

Sudden dread. Why was he asking her when she'd be home? Laura sat up. And scattered her work more in the process. "Irving, where are you? This minute. As we speak." Her insides curdled. "Oh. You used your key. You're at my place." Wordless moments passed during which she had time to wonder at the quirky mental makeup of a man who'd wonder if it was snowing only blocks away from where he was. Then, hearing the silence at the other end, she blurted, "Why, Irving? Why are you at my place?"

Why, Irving, why? What have I ever done to you?

She listened to his explanation. He and Vivian were fussing, and she'd left him. Well, made him bring her here. This was absolutely the last thing Laura needed. Her bickering family. Could the timing be worse? "Oh, yes. I'm surprised. Very surprised. What? Oh, yes…happy, too. Happy to see you both, that is. Not happy that you're having trouble. And Irving, why *are* you guys having trouble?"

Before he could say a word, Laura ordered, "Listen to me. I don't care what you did—or what she did— you two make up right now and get back to Rhode Island before you're snowed in with me." *And I therefore have to end my life in some bloody and dramatic way.* "What? You're fussing about whether or not she's psychic?"

Laura raked a hand through her hair and grimaced. "Tell her she is, Irving. Tell her. No, do not leave her here. No, Irving. There'll be another train. Don't leave her. I know you need to get home to Esther. She's with Cindy? Good. Go. But take Vivian with you, Irving. I—''

''Hello, Mother. Yes, I heard the door slam. So he's gone, huh? And you're still there? Well, that's just... *The last straw, the beginning of Armageddon, a disaster of Titanic proportions.* ''Peachy, Mother. Absolutely pea— Yes, I know my place is a mess. No, I wasn't burglarized. Yes, the sofa bed's out and there's a drawer sitting by my bed. I know all that, Mother. I had company. Yes, one of them was a baby.'' Laura covered her face with a hand. She knew when she was defeated. ''I'll tell you who and why later, okay? Yes, just make yourself at home. I'll be there as soon as I can. I love you, too.''

And then she hung up the receiver, sat cross-legged on her desk and stared at the phone. *Just shoot me now.*

GRANT GAVE the taxi driver Laura's address and turned his attention to the baby perched on his lap.

''So, Tucker, at least the whole day hasn't been a complete bust, huh, buddy? Imagine a snowstorm shutting down the Big Apple,'' Grant continued, as if expecting Tucker to hold up his end of the conversation. ''Yes, the airports are closed. You want to know a secret?'' Grant leaned in close to Tucker and whispered, ''Before now, I thought even the weather bent to my father's will.'' He straightened. ''But I guess not, huh?''

Tucker gave him the raspberries.

''My sentiments exactly,'' Grant soberly assured him. ''See, if all the players couldn't make it into town, then there couldn't be any coronation. So we're off the hook until this time next week. As it stands now, I don't work anywhere, Tucker. You and me, we're free men. Now don't look at me like that. I don't want to go see my folks at the Plaza. Why rattle that cage?''

Why, indeed. Grant huffed out his breath. Why spoil a fun afternoon by spending it answering countless questions about Tucker? And about Laura. A fun afternoon? Out in a blizzard with everything shutting down? You bet. He'd had a great time after learning the meeting had been canceled. And this from a guy who'd done some pretty adventurous things in his life. Skiing in the Alps. Yachting in the Mediterranean. Backpacking across Europe. Carnivale in Rio. To name a few. But none of those things could compare to the soul-satisfying afternoon he'd spent outfitting Tucker in the latest styles.

He laughed just thinking about it. The staff at Bloomie's had been more than happy to put off closing early to help him out. And the saleswoman had been pretty amused at his awkwardness with Tucker, although the baby didn't seem to appreciate it. But they'd totally bought his story of leaving home without making sure the diaper bag—Laura's woven grocery bag—had been fully packed to explain why he had no coat or clothes for the baby with him.

At the end of it all, they'd assured him that they would keep his visit with his godson hush-hush. Yes. Godson. A quick lie forced on him because Tucker had insisted on calling him da-da…repeatedly.

Even so, Grant knew there was little hope of the sales staff keeping quiet. They'd tell everyone they knew. Oh, well, another Grant Maguire sighting to add to his list, he told himself as he pushed over the ton of shopping bags and settled Tucker more comfortably on his lap. He focused on the fat, fuzzy, bunny-looking creature

Tucker now was, outfitted in his new sky-blue snowsuit. A suit he hated. And he'd let everyone in the store know in no uncertain and howling terms. Only the baby's rosy-cheeked little face was visible. And his expression wasn't pretty.

Grant couldn't help laughing. "Yeah, you hate this suit, don't you? Well, it serves you right. Call *me* dada, will you?"

Tucker pursed his little lips and said, "Da-da."

Grant nodded. "I hear you. What's wrong? Don't like fifty females fussing over you? Better get used to that. Because I think you're going to be a lady-killer." Tucker screwed his face up even more. "You look just like Laura when you do that."

At the mention of Laura, Tucker's blue eyes brightened. "Mama."

Grant slumped, hugging the boy to his chest. "I know how you feel. I perk right up, too, when I think about her. We're a couple of saps, aren't we? And here we don't even know if she wants either one of us."

As he held Tucker to him, Grant felt the baby snuggle sleepily against him. He settled himself, providing the little boy a still place to rest his head. Then, with his mind troubled and yet at peace—never had Grant felt so close to some sort of resolution in his life, only to have it stolen right out of his grasp—he exhaled and watched the people and the traffic struggling by. After a few minutes of that, he looked at Tucker and saw he was asleep. Grant's heart melted. *Could this be any harder?* His arms automatically and protectively encircled the baby bundle on his lap.

What was going on here? He meant with this baby. The abandonment scenario he and Laura had come up with, while certainly the most logical, didn't explain everything. Like that Tucker the Bear logo on the boy's sleeper. How did that get there? And why had Tucker taken so readily to Laura and to him? And them to him? Maybe Laura was right. Maybe Tucker *had* dropped out of the sky—part of some grand design. And for some good and cosmic reason that had to do with fate, with the two...well, three of them belonging together.

It wasn't the first time Grant had considered the idea. But it was the first time he'd wanted it to be true. He did. He wanted Laura. He wanted all of her. The good, the bad, even the morning grumpy. He chuckled and gave up. He was ready to walk over hot coals for her. Or through a blinding blizzard, given today's weather. He grinned again. So maybe it was true about Tucker. Maybe the baby was heaven-sent, as outlandish as that seemed. Outlandish maybe. And yet completely possible. If you believed.

Grant shook his head in wonder. *Well, then, so be it.* And it was then that he knew, somewhere deep in his heart, that his life, his happiness, rested in Laura's sweet hands. But beyond that, his life was also tangled up with this baby, too—for the rest of his life, no matter how it ended. *And end it would.* Reality crashed around Grant. *Face it now,* the voice said.

For despite how much he wanted it to be otherwise, the reality was Tucker had at least one parent out there somewhere. One who could come and claim him at any moment. Well, if that was the case, Grant vowed, his heart sinking at the very thought, he'd do his best to stay close to this child, just as he'd wished all his growing-up years for someone, a loving adult, to be there for him. Well, he hadn't had that. And he'd gotten over it.

But—and this Grant swore then and there—Tucker would know what it was like to be first. He'd know what it was like to be loved by the most important people in his life. And he'd never have to get over it. Nor would he be a statistic. Or a cliché. Never would he wear a label, a tag. Poor little rich boy. Underprivileged youth. No. Not this child. Not if it was in Grant's power to prevent it. And he felt sure it was, that he could prevent it. How?

One word. Money. Grant had learned that early on. It didn't buy happiness, but it had insulated him from some of life's harsher realities. He'd never had to wonder where his next meal was coming from or where he'd rest for the night. That security was what he'd give Tucker...should the baby's real mother show up to blow Grant's whole heaven-sent theory. At the very least, he told himself, he could do some good with his money. He could make sure that the boy had everything he needed.

Just as this snowsuit insulated and protected the baby physically, Grant vowed to do the same for the boy emotionally. But not only with money. Money was a means. Nothing more. What Tucker needed in his life was Grant's love, his involvement and his influence— *Wait.* Suddenly an idea swirled in Grant's mind. The idea was so simple, and yet so right, that it made him damned sorry he hadn't been able to sign on the dotted line today just thinking of the good he could do. Not only for Tucker, but for a lot of children.

Amazed at his idea, Grant sat up straighter, seeing the world as a brighter place. And himself as a better person. All because of one baby. He looked at Tucker, helpless, trusting, asleep on his lap. Grant's heart tore with the tenderness he felt. So, no matter whether the baby was heaven-sent or Earth-born, Grant would be there for him. No matter who he lived with.

Who he lived with. That thought brought Grant around to Laura again. As much as he wanted to—as much as he wanted to smell her womanly scent, see her smile, hear her voice—why was he going to her place? For one thing—and a practical thing it was—what made him think she'd be home? If she wasn't, he didn't have a key. Well, he supposed he could call her office on his cell phone to see where she was. He felt the phone's weight against his hip as it rested in his overcoat pocket. To get to it, he'd have to disturb Tucker. Grant looked at the angelic sleeping little boy. No, thank you. He would just as soon have poked a stick at a rabid rottweiler.

And what about Laura? Despite his feelings for her, he didn't really know where he stood with her. You can love someone all you want, but if they don't return your feelings, what good does it do you? Hell, he didn't even know if she wanted to see him again. Or the baby. After all, her plan had been to take Tucker to the authorities before they got nailed for keeping him. Grant again looked at the trusting little boy on his lap, leaning against his heart…in more ways than one. Well, put that way, knowing what to do was easy, wasn't it?

Because what he felt for Laura was one thing. And what he felt for Tucker was another. His responsibilities to the one weren't the same as what he owed the other. Laura wasn't helpless, but the baby was. *So, Grant, what's so easy about it?* Nothing, he admitted. Why was he thinking of taking care of Tucker by himself for the next few days? What did he know about taking care of a baby? Into his mind flashed yesterday's diaper-changing fiasco at Cohn and Draper. Hell, he'd almost dropped the kid twice.

And then there'd been the fiasco this morning after

Laura left them alone and trotted off to work. It had taken him two horrifying hours to get himself and Tucker ready to go out. And still he wasn't sure if he'd permanently warped the kid's little psyche by sitting him in his infant carrier and putting him in the shower with him. What choice had he had? Where else could he put the little scooting machine while he bathed? And who knew that, when wet, babies were as slippery as greased seals? They'd both ended up sudsy and sitting—and laughing—on the shower's tiled floor before it was all done.

As if that weren't enough of a wake-up call, there'd been the episode in Bloomie's just now. It had taken him and three knowledgable women to get Tucker and all his movable parts into this snowsuit getup. How the hell was he supposed to get him out of it by himself? The mere thought made Grant break out in a sweat. Tucker had eyed him as if Grant would drop him...and with good reason, Grant admitted.

Laura, as inept as she may be, at least had brothers and sisters. She knew what it was like to have munchkins around. But not Grant. Everything had always been done for him by nannies and nurses and butlers and maids. Grant frowned, wondering if maybe he should hire a nanny. No. Hadn't he just said he wanted to be involved? Well, here was his chance. He could be involved right up to his elbows. With this little boy. Wasn't that what he'd decided only moments ago? May as well start proving it, then. To Tucker. To Laura. And especially to himself.

With that decision, Grant leaned forward enough to tap the cabbie on the shoulder and get his attention. "I've changed my mind. Turn around." He gave his own address to the man.

IN LAURA'S LIVING ROOM, her mother leaned her ample bulk forward on the blue-checked slipcovered chair. "You're telling me that just like that—" Vivian made a snapping noise with her long red-lacquered fingernails "—you have a baby?"

"Yes." Sitting on the sofa, her jeans-clad legs drawn up on the cushions, Laura fiddled with her socks and felt like she was ten years old again as she avoided direct eye contact with her mother. "Well, not actually yes. It's more like no. But only sort of. I guess."

Then, feeling nothing like Madison Avenue's high-powered, goal-oriented wunderkind—but forgiving herself with the thought that who *did* live up to the public's view of them when faced with their mother's questioning scrutiny—Laura finally looked up. And saw Vivian pushing her frizzy, black hair from her heavily rouged face. "Which is it, honey? Do you or don't you have a baby? I need to know so I can worry."

"Okay, I do. But it's not mine, so you don't need to worry."

"I don't need to worry? Talk to me about Frederick, your brother."

Laura couldn't believe this. "We were just kids. That was years ago."

"Oh? Then why's he still afraid of clothes dryers? The man is in his twenties and can't walk through the major appliances center in department stores. I should've grounded you for that until you were thirty-five."

Laura tried not to laugh, but didn't succeed. "I was just trying to dry his clothes."

"With him still in them, for God's sake?"

"Well, we didn't want to get into trouble for going down to that creek."

"Where you almost drowned him."

"So how did I know the sink-or-swim method doesn't always have a happy ending? Come on, Mother, I told you—I was a kid."

"A kid? Can we talk about Esther and the elevator five years ago? When you left her in there? I should've whipped your behind for that one, grown woman or no. But thank God she came out okay. And Cindy—that dog you stuck her on, telling her it was a pony? She had to have shots. Remember that?"

Laura stared at her mother and thought of everything she'd just said. "Maybe you're right. But still, with this baby, it's not what you think, Mother."

Vivian cocked her head and raised her dramatically darkened eyebrows. "Don't tell me what I think. I'm the one who's psychic. Not you."

Laura rolled her eyes. "All right, Mother, if you're so psychic, then you tell me what's going on here."

Accepting the challenge, Vivian closed her eyes and massaged her temples. Almost immediately she straightened, opened her eyes and flopped her bejeweled fingers onto her flower-skirted lap. "It's no use. I can't. First Irving's fussing with me. And now all that snow outside. Too much static in my head. Like the snow on TV. It interferes with the mind's pathways."

Begrudgingly impressed, Laura stared at her mother. Even from that far out on a limb, the woman had come back. Vivian was good. Very good. But not that good....
"Tell me I'm adopted," Laura begged.

Vivian pursed her orange-lipsticked mouth. "I'd like to, but you know good and well I'm your biological mother. And I have the scars—emotional and physical—to prove it. So tell me, Miss Smarty-pants—and I'm almost afraid to ask here—where is this baby?"

Laura's heart tugged. She'd give anything to know where Tucker was. And where Grant was. The two of them. Together. But still, this was an opening, one Laura couldn't resist. She grinned evilly and looked at her watch. "Hey, he should be back about now. I sent him out to the grocery for more—"

Vivian's fearful squawk was coupled with the intercom's buzzing and Laura's leaping off the sofa, right over its upholstered back. "Maybe that's him," she yelled, to tease her mother.

But in her heart she knew it had to be Grant. No one else would be out on a day like this. Indeed, no one she knew had any reason to drop by. Scrambling in a sock-sliding tear across the hardwood floors, her heart hammering and hopeful, she skittered across the room, throwing her words over her shoulder. "I'm just kidding, Mother. Maybe it's Gra—" Oops. She hadn't mentioned Grant yet. She slid, shoulder first, to a stop by the doors and pushed the button. "Yes?" But she missed the answer because...

Right at her elbow, her mother said, "A baby that can go to the grocery and push an intercom button? That's a big baby. I gotta see this kid."

Laura made a pleading face at Vivian. "Mother, please. I missed who—" The intercom buzzed again. Laura turned to the machine, pushed the button again and said, "Hello?"

"Mrs. Sloan?" a friendly-sounding female voice asked.

Laura's heart sank. Obviously, it wasn't Grant. But Mrs. Sloan? *Who would think I'm married—dear God, the authorities.* Her insides froze. She met but didn't answer her mother's questioning expression. "Yes?" Laura ventured into the speaker.

"Mrs. Sloan, my name is Linda Gibson. I'm with Child Protective Services. I'm here about Baby Doe."

That was all she said, but it was enough to melt Laura's bones. She wanted to sink to the floor and die. *Oh, sure, now they get it straight. Now they realize I have the baby. Sort of.* Yeah, now, when her mother was here. And now, when she had no idea where Baby Doe was. Can you say go straight to jail, do not pass go, do not collect two hundred dollars?

"Laura?" her mother whispered, pinching her arm and eliciting a squeal of pain from her. "Say something to the nice lady. It's freezing outside."

Laura snapped to the moment and nodded at Vivian. Then, speaking into the intercom, she said, "Um, hold on. I'll buzz you up." Then she grabbed her mother by both arms and squeezed hard. "Oh, my God, *think,* Mother. What can I tell them? I don't have any idea where the baby is. We'll have to lie."

"Laura Elizabeth Sloan, what have I told you about lying?"

Even rattled, Laura could spout her mother's pearls of wisdom. "Make the lie short, because not only is the truth stranger than fiction, it's also shorter. And keep a straight face when you're telling it."

"Good girl," Vivian said, patting her. "Now where is the baby?"

"Grant took him."

A wordless moment passed, then Vivian exploded. "I *knew* I heard you say Grant when I called you. Grant *Maguire?* It is him, isn't it?" Her mother's bright-eyed wonderment and hopeful grin unnerved Laura. "And there really *is* a baby?"

"Yes. And yes. I'll explain later. But not now, Mother. I may be going to jail here any minute—"

Vivian's expression fell. "Jail? What have you done, Laura? Who's Baby Doe, anyway?"

"We don't know, Mother. That's why they call him Baby Doe. But I call him Tucker."

"You do? Why?"

"Because when I found him," Laura heard herself idiotically explaining to Vivian, "he had on a sleeper with a Tucker the Bear logo on the front. And that's the company Grant—" Laura clapped a hand over her mouth, stared at her mother, then grabbed her again. "Mother, it doesn't matter why. The important thing here is I don't know where the baby is. Do you hear me? I. Do. Not. Know. Where. The. Baby. Is. And the nice lady coming up right now isn't going to be happy to hear that."

She stared into Vivian's widening eyes and waited for realization to sink in. When it did, when her mother's lipsticked mouth dropped open, Laura nodded. "Exactly. Help me, Mother. Or I'm going to jail."

Before Vivian could respond, the doorbell rang. Laura stared into her mother's eyes. The baby wasn't here. Grant wasn't here. But the moment of truth was. And it called for a big, fat, whopping lie.

6

"WE GAVE HIM BACK to his real mother."

We what? Laura could only stare at her straight-faced mother and will her heart to quit spasming as she closed the door behind Ms. Gibson.

Linda Gibson, an attractive African-American woman of about thirty-five, stopped dead in the act of unwrapping herself from her winter coat, having pretty much the same reaction as Laura. "You what?"

"We gave him back," Vivian repeated, still straight-faced.

"You gave the baby back to his *real* mother?" Ms. Gibson repeated, frowning in a way that didn't bode well for Laura. She cut her gaze to Laura, who managed a tight smile that didn't show any teeth. "How'd you know it was his real mother?"

Laura blinked at Ms. Gibson and turned to her accomplished liar of a mother. "You heard the lady. She asked you how we knew it was his real mother."

Vivian shot her a go-along-with-me glare and smoothed her features. "Don't you remember, honey? She—she had his birth certificate."

"His birth certificate?" Ms. Gibson repeated, her voice flat. "It could have been *any* baby's birth certificate. Or a forged document. But besides that, the only thing it proves is she has a birth certificate for a baby.

Not necessarily for *that* baby, Mrs.—I'm sorry, I didn't get your name."

"Smith," Vivian smoothly replied. Laura stared at her mother, Mrs. Irving Pendergast. *Smith?*

"Mrs. Smith," Ms. Gibson repeated. Her disbelief was obvious in her raised eyebrow, the grim set of her mouth. "I'm afraid we have a very big problem here. A big legal problem. With your names on it. That baby was entrusted to you by the state—"

"No, he wasn't," Laura interrupted, fearing to let Ms. Gibson go any further with this but more afraid that Vivian Smith would murky the waters. "I took him to the police the minute I found him, and they took my name and address. Which is how you knew to come here. And they told me to take him home—"

"They *what?*" Finally! Ms. Gibson seemed to realize somebody *else* had screwed up.

"Well, in so many words," Laura continued. "At any rate, they didn't take him from me. I'm not sure they even knew I had him with me. But anyway, I brought him home. And the policeman at the desk said I'd be contacted. And I was—an officer came by this morning. But again with the story wrong. So, the way I see it, I have complied with the law, I've done everything I was told. And I've simply waited. Again, as directed." Laura coupled her words with a direct stare.

The next one who spoke...lost.

Ms. Gibson seemed to understand that. She stared back, her gaze shifting from Laura to Mrs. Smith and back to Laura. She slumped. "All right. You're right. I just got the case myself, and I have to admit, the paperwork was a mess. So, I say we just go forward from here, okay?"

Laura exhaled, weak with relief. "Whew. Okay. Good. I'm glad you're so reasonable."

Ms. Gibson smiled and nodded at Laura. "I'm that, if nothing else. So, from everything you just said, I gather you didn't really give the baby away to a stranger claiming to be his mother. Is that right?"

Finally. A chance to tell the truth. Without looking at and thereby further implicating her mother, Laura said, "Yes."

"Good." It was Ms. Gibson's turn to exhale in relief as she looked around the open loft. "So where is Baby Doe—really?"

"I don't know," Laura confessed, drawing the caseworker's instant scrutiny. She quickly added, "It's not like it sounds. I may not know where he is, but I do know with whom he is." Laura frowned. *With whom? Is that right?* "Or who has him. Anyway, he's not a stranger. And the baby is fine." *I hope,* Laura added, mentally crossing her fingers as she thought of Grant's total lack of experience with kids.

"I certainly hope so," Ms. Gibson echoed. "So, who's he with? And why?"

The why of it Laura didn't really want to get into. And then it hit her, as the wordless seconds stretched out, the name she was going to have to give. Ms. Gibson would think she was lying. Again. She may as well say King Arthur, for all she was going to be believed. *Grant Maguire? Yeah, right. Ha, ha.* Laura could hear her now, could envision this nice lady dialing the police. But what else could Laura do? She swallowed and said, "Grant—"

"Smith," Vivian broke in. "Grant Smith."

Along with Laura, Ms. Gibson eyed Vivian, looking her up and down. Laura cringed inside. She was used to her mother's affected and outlandish appearance, but most people who resided in the sane world weren't. Sure enough, the caseworker's eyebrows rose. "Grant Smith, huh? A relative, I presume?"

"Yes," Vivian said.

At the same time Laura said, "No."

Ms. Gibson eyed them both and finished unbuttoning her coat as she turned to Laura. "I don't know what's going on here. But we've got to get to the bottom of it. So put some water in the kettle. We're going to need some strong, hot tea. And a nice, long *truthful* chat. Because— Well, let me tell you what I'm doing out on a bitter day like today when all my colleagues have been sent home. You see, *I* have Baby Doe's *real* mother waiting at the precinct for her son to be returned to her. And I'm not leaving here without him."

WHO KNEW *babies had this many moving parts,* Grant wondered, as Tucker fussed at him while he tried to disentangle the boy from the snowsuit. "You know," Grant informed the baby, "this would be a lot easier if you'd quit— See? That's what I'm talking about. Quit trying to roll over, okay? This damn—excuse me— *darned* thing has as many zippers and snaps as a sleeping bag. It's bad enough you had to eat in it. And you're not helping any—"

"Da-da," Tucker howled. "Da-da, da-da, da-da!" As if that were a call to action, he neatly flipped over and broke a few land speed records as he scooted away, his half-off, half-deconstructed and dangling snowsuit following him like a snake's partially shed skin. Grant never stood a chance of grabbing him. Tucker was already rounding a table.

"Ah, damm—doggone it." Grant chuckled as he

sprawled on the thickly carpeted floor of his upper Manhattan apartment. He rested his hands on his thighs and watched as Tucker stopped and peered at him over his shoulder. "I'm not going to chase you. Not this time," Grant assured the baby, knowing he already had four other times, which had pretty much elevated this activity to the status of a game.

Tucker took a moment to digest this, or to assess Grant's seriousness—who knew with babies?—and rolled to a sitting position, his chubby little legs out in front of him, his snowsuit twisted and dangling from his ankles. He pointed to Grant. "Da-da."

"Nice try." Grant folded his arms over his chest. He wasn't buying the da-da bit this time. Not with baby cereal dripping from his lacquered kitchen cabinets. Not with formula cans and plastic bottles and rubber nipples littering the counters and the floor. And not with a snowsuit confounding the life out of him. "Can't you say anything else besides da-da?"

As if he understood Grant's words and the concept of a joke, Tucker grinned. "Mama."

"Thanks." Grant's heart tugged, as he reached for and rolled a hard-rubber ball to Tucker. *Laura.* He'd give anything to see her right now. He still wasn't sure why he hadn't called her, why he hadn't let her know he...well, the baby anyway...was fine. After all, here it was late afternoon. And a blizzard was raging outside. She had to be concerned. It wasn't from stubbornness that he hadn't contacted her, Grant defended himself. He just hadn't had a chance since he got home a couple hours ago. Grant watched Tucker pick up the ball and—what else?—try to put it in his mouth.

Scrambling on all fours and crawling toward the baby, before he swallowed it, Grant wondered how in the world single parents managed. This was insane. When did they eat? Sleep? Read? Go to the bathroom? Or did they just lock themselves in the bathroom and do all those things there? Grant eased the red ball from the baby's mouth and held onto him as he pulled the snowsuit free of his legs. Both booties went with it. "Great."

Grant fished them out of the snowsuit legs, tugged them onto the fat little feet of the suddenly still and cooperative, seriously intent and red-faced Tucker. "There. At last, my man—freedom!" And then he smelled it. Grant's expression, along with his mood, crumpled. He sat on his haunches, completely disenchanted, and stared at the relieved-looking blue-eyed baby. "Ah, come on, man. Not again. Not the toxic diaper. How do you make so much—"

The intercom buzzed insistently and persistently. Frowning, Grant looked at the baby and shrugged. Tucker raised an eyebrow. "You expecting anybody?" Grant asked him.

"Mama," Tucker said, his blue eyes bright, his candycane-sweet little voice all but breathless.

"Yeah, right. Don't we wish." Grant picked Tucker up, holding him in front of him as he headed for the door. Once there, he tucked the baby under his arm like he would a football, like he'd seen Laura do, and pushed the button. "Yes, Mr. Dunkel?"

"Evening, Mr. Maguire," the doorman responded. "Sorry to bother you, sir. But I have a frantic young lady down here who insists I call you. Says her name is—"

Mr. Dunkel yelped, his cry followed closely by some sort of garbled melee. Then silence. Grant exchanged a look with Tucker, who grimaced. Then a different voice came over the intercom. "I don't have time for this. Grant? This is Laura. You tell this guy it's okay for me to come up. I mean it. We've got trouble. Big trouble."

Laura? Trouble? Synonymous, at best. Grant stared at the speaker on the wall, then at the smug baby tucked under his arm. "How'd you know?" he asked the child. But Tucker wasn't telling. Grant turned toward the speaker. "Mr. Dunkel?" *If you're still conscious.* "It's all right. I know her. She can come up."

Grant heard Laura say, "See? I told you I knew him. As if I'm some thrill-seeking groupie of the Magnificant Mr.—"

The intercom went dead. Grant stepped back, staring at it. And chuckled. He hoped it had gone dead because Mr. Dunkel had recovered enough to hit the Off button. Then Grant remembered, thanks to his keen sense of smell, the stinky baby under his arm. Wrinkling his nose in distaste, he shifted his weight and his grip and successfully manuevered the uncomplaining child in front of him. Staring into the baby's blinking blue eyes, Grant said, "So, what do you think this big trouble is, huh? It's just a guess here, but I'm thinking it's something to do with you."

To which Tucker replied, "Damn."

THE ELEVATOR CAR couldn't rise rapidly enough. Its two doors couldn't open quickly enough. Laura quickly stepped out and strode down the oak wainscoted, carpeted hall. She fought the scarf that all but choked her, and tugged off her woolen cap, then ran her fingers through her hair and looked from one side of the long, curving hallway to the other, looking for Grant's apartment.

About the time she decided she was lost, there it was.

Well, there Grant was, anyway, standing in the hall, a doorway behind him. Grant and the baby. A part of Laura slumped in relief. *Thank God, the baby.* Obviously her fears were unfounded, because man and baby both appeared fine. She focused on Grant. *Oh, yeah, so fine. Good job, God.*

And yet, there was another part of her that wanted to cry. *Oh, no. Grant and the baby. I could lose them both tonight.* Tucker would be returned to his parents. *You knew this was coming, Laura,* she told herself sternly. But what about Grant? Would he stick around once Tucker was no longer the glue bonding them together? Or would he run? The same way he'd done before, and at a time when their love was an acknowledged thing between them? Unlike it was now. In only a few moments, he could be gone again. Just like Tucker. And she'd be without them.

"Laura," Grant called. "Is my doorman still alive?"

She shrugged noncommittally and quirked her mouth. "I think he'd meet the clinical definition."

Grant's wide and answering grin, the warm expression on his face and his arm held out to her, open invitations for her to walk into his embrace, eclipsed all else. That and Tucker's squeal of delight upon seeing her. It was like a cruel hoax. Especially given the task she was here to perform, and the conflict warring between her heart and her head.

But maybe some optimism was exactly what she needed. She'd never seen two more welcome faces than Grant's and Tucker's. She put her doubts aside and stepped into Grant's embrace, hugging him, breathing in his wonderfully warm and masculine scent—along with a diabolically acrid one strong enough to make her eyes bleed. Laura jerked out of Grant's embrace and held her scarf and woolen cap over her nose. "Oh, my God, what is that?"

"Your next project," Grant quipped, jerking a thumb in the baby's direction. "Come on in. You can help me change him while you tell me about this big trouble we've got."

Stuffing her cap and scarf in a deep coat pocket, Laura took a step backward. "I don't think so. About the diaper, I mean."

"Oh, but I do," Grant drawled and grinned, managing to look devilishly handsome in the dim light of the hallway. "It's only fair. I've changed two already. So the joy is now yours, ma'am."

"Lucky me," Laura quipped, her expression as sour as the chore awaiting her.

Tucker continued to beam and chortle, his pudgy little hands held out to Laura, his blue eyes bright with anticipation as he leaned toward her and chanted, "Mama, mama, mama, mama."

"I think he wants you," Grant said, his eyes warming, his expression softening. "I know I do."

And that was when Laura lost it. "Oh, Grant," she moaned as tears stung her eyes. "Why are you saying that now?"

"Why not? What's wrong with now? What's happened, Laura?"

"Can't you guess?" she challenged as she grabbed the baby, stinky britches and all, and held him to her. It took a moment for her to realize she'd never seen the sailboat-appliquéd jumpsuit he wore. She pinched the fabric between her fingers and asked, "Where'd he get this?"

"My noon meeting was canceled until next week. So

us guys went shopping. Got a lot of good loot. And about a thousand unsolicited baby-care tips, too.''

Laura nodded, hoping her expression revealed only interest. Because she was thinking, *I missed a shopping excursion?* Somehow that hurt. And made her feel out of the loop. Then Grant got quiet and stared at her, as if trying to see into her soul. Or maybe read her thoughts. Uncomfortable with such close scrutiny, she quickly responded, ''That sounds like big fun.''

Grant blinked, then looked into her eyes and said, ''Not big fun. In case you're wondering—'' he pointed to Tucker ''—not a fun shopping date.''

Laura finally grinned. ''Typical guy, huh?''

Grant smiled. ''I wouldn't know. But anyway, I guess we need to talk about what brings you here,'' he said, sounding as if he already had it figured out and hated it. ''I should have called you earlier, but I…well, I—''

''Really. It's okay. It's been crazy,'' she said, letting him off the hook. She buried her nose in Tucker's fat, soft baby neck. And tried not to cry. But it didn't work. Tucker clutched at her, nosing her cheek and jaw as if trying to bestow innocent little kisses on her. That did it. Laura was sobbing. She felt Grant put his hand on her shoulder, rubbing it up and down her coat-covered arm as if in sympathy. Which only made things worse. Because Tucker began bawling, too.

''All right, that's it,'' Grant pronounced as he herded Laura and the baby into his apartment. Closing the door behind them, making it no farther than the tiled foyer, he put his arms around them both and kissed first Laura's forehead and then Tucker's. ''So, why is everybody crying?'' he asked.

The baby quieted as Laura looked at Grant. Before she could say a word, he bent over her and kissed her on the mouth. It was a comforting little peck, almost as innocent as Tucker's efforts a moment ago. Laura surprised herself by returning it as if it were the most natural thing. Then she sniffed back a sob and said, "There's a caseworker—"

"A caseworker?" Grant pulled back, grimacing. "Oh, no."

Laura nodded. "Oh, yes. Anyway, she's at my place with my mother—"

Grant stiffened. "Your mother? But why's she—"

"Grant, please," Laura implored, shifting the baby and squeezing Grant's arm in a gesture that begged him to allow her to finish. "This is hard enough. Just listen, okay?" She took a deep breath…and nearly choked. "Can we change him before I pass out?"

Grant jumped into action, taking Tucker from her. "Oh, sure. I'm sorry. Follow me."

Laura walked after him, shedding her coat as she took in the designer-showroom yet comfortable opulence of Grant's private world. All high ceilings and polished woods and huge vases and big pictures and overstuffed furniture, right through the carpeted living room, down a short hallway, past a wallpapered bathroom and into the lion's den. His bedroom. Massive. Rich. Masculine. Inviting. Just like the man. Laura stopped, trying to imagine herself in this world. His world.

Despite the trouble they were in, despite the heartache brewing within her, she took a moment to look around, to appreciate her surroundings and to assure herself that… *I could do this. Wow.* She tossed her coat on the thick, gold-quilted bedspread and perched gingerly on the king-size bed's edge, crossing her legs and pretending to be at home.

Grant knelt next to the bed and placed the stinky baby

on a big maroon towel on the thick carpet. Champagne-colored carpet, no less. Laura sighed, focusing on Grant and seeing that he hadn't lied. His practiced motions said he'd done this before. And he was armed. Disposable diapers, baby wipes, baby outfits, various toys and a much-squeezed tube of baby ointment were strewn around the towel, somehow making the scene look like a declared disaster area.

Grant evidently remembered she was supposed to be helping. He looked at her, held Tucker down with a hand splayed across the child's naked little belly and crooked a finger her way. "Come here."

Laura edged backward on the bed. "I'll give you a thousand dollars not to make me."

Grant chuckled. "I don't need the money. Come here."

Disgusted, Laura stood, already shoving up her sweater's sleeves as she kneeled to join him before the baby. "So. What can I do to help?" she said, all saccharine sweetness as she got ready to follow orders.

Orders Grant was all too ready to give. "Hand me a wipe there. Yeah. Just pop it up. Like that. Thanks. Okay, two more. Whoa. This kid is the champ, isn't he? Whew. Okay…all clean. Now the ointment…like so. There we go. And then we put the diaper and do the tapes like so. Hold still, Tucker. Okay, there you go. Here. Take this, Laura. Oh, stop it. It won't bite. Just toss it…hell, I don't know where—out a window. Damn. Phew."

"Phew," Tucker repeated, grimacing and waving his chubby arms in the air.

Holding the incriminating evidence at arm's length, Laura walked stiff-legged to the bathroom Grant pointed to and found more fabulous opulence—gold fixtures and a marble shower and a sunken hot tub—and on the tiled floor a big plastic trash bag. Which she correctly guessed was for the diaper. She dumped the dirty work into it and got the heck out of there, only to watch Grant, still on his knees in the bedroom, finish doing up the leg snaps on Tucker's outfit—

While Tucker tried his best to turn over and crawl away. And Grant did his best to grab the baby and flip him onto his back. Time after time. Much to Tucker's squealing delight. "Looks like a game," Laura commented, grinning, drawing Grant's attention. And giving Tucker a chance to escape with one foot still hanging out from the sleeper.

"A big game. One I keep losing because—" Grant pointed to Tucker "—he won't tell me the rules." Her heart warming to this paternal side of Grant, Laura watched as he sat on his haunches, chuckling as he shook his head and watched the madcap baby jet around the bed and pull himself up, hanging onto the gold bedspread. He turned a bright-eyed stare on Grant and then Laura.

"Yeah, I see you," she laughingly assured Tucker, before focusing on Grant...only to catch him staring at her. He looked serious. Her countenance sobered. "What?"

Grant shrugged. "You just look... Well, it's good to see you again." Laura swallowed tightly. "I'm curious. About how you found me. Not that where I live is any big secret I'm trying to keep from you. In fact, I should've left my address at your place."

Laura nodded. Then, raking her hand through her hair and sending a doting glance toward Tucker, who moved with mincing little steps around the bed away from them, Laura said, "Let's just say that Big Brother is watching you. Meaning having an employee of the state on your side helps. Linda Gibson, Tucker's caseworker, got on the phone. But only after I'd convinced her that I wasn't lying when I told her who had Tucker. Well, anyway, it only took about ten seconds to have you pinpointed."

Grant frowned. "Doesn't surprise me, really. The cops keep up with me. I get a lot of harassment. Not that that's what you're doing. But you know what I mean. So. Why isn't this Linda Gibson here with you?"

"Are you kidding? It's like you said. You're Grant Maguire. And now that she believes me, she's not in too big a hurry to make a scene. Especially given how her official pals have screwed this matter up so far. She's more concerned that *you'll* kick up a fuss. So she's 'giving me this opportunity,' as she put it, to get Tucker back to her on my own."

Having told her tale—well, most of it—Laura glanced the baby's way just in time to see him disappear from view. Quite suddenly. No doubt he'd misstepped and sat down heavily. He didn't fuss, so she didn't worry. Turning her attention to Grant, she said, "There's more."

Grant chuckled, somehow lending a fatalistic note to the sound. "There's always more."

"Don't I know it. Anyway, Ms. Gibson says—" Laura stopped, suddenly overcome. She sniffed, swallowing around the growing lump in her throat and waiting a wordless moment to compose herself before—

"What does Ms. Gibson say, Laura?" Grant urged quietly.

Laura met his honey-eyed gaze and inhaled deeply, trying to counteract the emotional tightness in her chest.

"She says that Tucker's mother showed up at the precinct. We...we have to give him back. Tonight."

"Son of a—" Grant cut off his words and swiped his hand over his face. He looked away from her, staring at all the new things he'd bought Tucker. A tic in his jaw gave his feelings away. Laura felt sure she knew what was going through his mind. Because the same thoughts were running through hers, too, sitting there watching him stare at the purchases that had fueled his fantasy.

So, it was true. Grant had no more prepared himself psychologically for the baby's departure than she had. Weren't they just two of a kind? And wasn't it sad? Or perhaps "delusional" was a better word. Because all along, they'd known Tucker wasn't theirs, known they couldn't keep him. And yet look at them. *Yeah, look at us.*

Laura sat back, observing their situation as a stranger would, and considered their behavior. And realized that, overall, she liked who they were. *Gosh, we're good people to care this much about an abandoned baby, aren't we?* She blinked. They were, weren't they? And their working together *was* about the baby, wasn't it? Or was it more?

Grant exhaled and swung his gaze—now hard amber—to her. "All right. I guess I've just been kidding myself that— Well, it doesn't matter. Okay, we knew this was going to happen. And it's for the best, Laura. For Tucker's sake."

Who was he trying to convince? Himself or her? Then Laura realized she was shaking her head and that hot tears were coursing down her cheeks. "No."

"Yes," Grant countered. "He's not ours—I mean, yours. Or mine." He couldn't look her in the eye.

Seeming thoroughly demoralized, Grant swung his gaze the baby's way—well, where he'd been—and his frown deepened.

"He sat down." Laura sniffed.

"Oh," Grant said simply enough, settling on the carpet. He shot her a glance. "Did I hear you say earlier that your mother's here?"

She knew what he was doing. Changing the subject, helping her get through. Bringing up Vivian to lighten the moment, if not the load. And darn him, it was working. Laura let out an audible sigh as she wilted backward on Grant's bed, flopping an arm over her closed eyes. "Yes," she whined. "She and Irving are having a tiff. Remember that dumb saying about today being the first day of the rest of your life? Well, that was today. My whole life happened today, Grant. Everything. Just…boom. 'Hello, Laura, here we are, complication after complication. Are you having fun yet?'"

Grant's chuckle—the proximity of its sound to her and the sinking weight next to her—told her he'd joined her on the bed. Her spirits immediately picked up, as did her heart rate. She opened her eyes, turned her head to her left and saw him. He'd stretched out close to her, on his belly, his chin resting on his folded arms as he faced forward and grinned at… Laura flipped onto her belly and brushed her hair out of her eyes. Tucker. Curly black hair awry. Blue eyes bright. His little mouth opened wide in a grin. He'd obviously pulled himself up and was quite pleased with his efforts.

Seeing him, feeling Grant's warm body next to her and considering where she was, in Grant's bedroom with him and this baby, the emotional onslaught was just too much. Elation and giddiness warred with defeat and wretchedness. It was overwhelming. Determined to speak before her internal censor could stop her, Laura elbowed herself onto her side and looked Grant's way. "There's just one thing I have to say."

Grant edged his heavy-lidded gaze her way and reached out to smooth her cascading hair out of her face. "And what's that?"

Her senses fired by his touch, by his nearness, Laura waved a hand in a big lazy arc, indicating the whole scene. "This. It's right. The whole thing, Grant. Me. You. Tucker. Us here like this." She saw Grant's slow grin, his nod of agreement, and rushed on. "It is, isn't it? It's just...*right*. That's how it feels. I don't know how else to put it."

"You're doing fine," Grant assured her, cutting off her words by tugging her to him and kissing her speechless. A wet, moaning, openmouthed, kiss that Laura felt all the way from the top of her head, down her body and past her toes. In fact, she felt it all the way back to her fifth birthday.

When Grant broke away from her, perspiration coated her forehead. Grant's condition mirrored hers. After a moment during which they stared, shocked, yearning, only inches apart, into each other's eyes, Grant muttered, "We'll get through this, Laura. I swear it. We'll do this. Together."

And then? she wanted to ask him but didn't. In fact, she couldn't speak at all. Grant seemed to realize that as he slowly rubbed his hand up and down her arm. "I mean it. No matter what, we'll get through this, Laura. Now, about Tucker. If we—" He stopped, looked grim and tried again. "There's no if to it, is there? *When* we give him back—"

"No."

Grant's mouth was open, but no words came out. He

stared wide-eyed at Laura. She returned him look for look. Because she hadn't said a word. Together they turned to the speaker. Tucker. Apparently not wanting to be left out, determined to have a say in his own future, the little boy pointed at them and said, "Mama. Da-da."

Laura exchanged another look with Grant. Then they swung their gazes to the baby. "You don't want to go back, do you?" Grant said.

Tucker shook his little head and said, plain as day, "No."

7

"WELL, what do we do now, Grant?" Exasperation was obvious in Laura's voice.

Grant was just as frustrated. "About what? Our taxi being stuck in a traffic jam, when it'd be quicker to get out and walk—if we didn't mind freezing to death, along with the baby? Or about the power outage that knocked out the streetlights? Or are you talking about the caseworker waiting at your place? Or maybe about your mother being there, too? And what about my parents being in town? Or, hey, let's not forget about Tucker's not wanting to go back to his mother? Then there's me and you—"

"That's right. All of it. I don't like any of it." Laura thought for a moment and frowned. "Except about me and you. I like that part." She whacked his arm a good one. "But only if you do."

"Well, fine. Because I do. I like it." But sitting in the back seat of a taxi, stuck in the hopelessly snarled traffic, Grant didn't look all that happy about it, Laura decided.

But still, somewhere deep inside, she took heart. "Good. Me, too."

"Fine." He spit the words out.

"Fine."

And then it got quiet. Laura stared straight ahead, blinking, hating that they'd sniped at each other. Why had she started it? They both had their hands full. Not only did they have Tucker, as well as his shockingly big and fully stuffed diaper bag. But in the larger sense, they were in this together.

Laura slumped, accepting their snit as an exchange you could only have with someone you knew well and cared about. It was true. Only people who were involved, who knew what was going on with each other, could say those things. Okay, it was small comfort. But comfort nonetheless.

She looked at the warm bundle in her lap and decided to enjoy the silence. Well, silence was a relative term. In this case it excluded the rude and happy sounds coming from the snow-bunny-suited Tucker as he sat facing her and picking at a big wooden button on her coat. Three times already she'd had to stop him from trying to pull it into his mouth.

Remembering Tucker's antics brought a smile to Laura's face—her first since they'd left Grant's place. They'd spent ten harrowing minutes stuck in the elevator when the power blinked off. That had been fun. Big fun. But they'd survived. The electricity had come back on, unfortunately not before Mr. Dunkel had a chance to save them by attempting to pry open the doors—with a crowbar, of all things. She knew the creepy little doorman had loved that, getting to feel superior. Especially after the way she'd yelled at him earlier. Among other things.

Rolling her eyes, dismissing the adventure, she focused on Tucker, lovingly rubbing the baby's well-padded back. The sweet little guy was blessedly oblivious, or seemingly so—who knew with him?—to the problems swirling over his sky-blue-hooded head. He had to be. Because here he sat singing. Well, not singing so much as testing his vocal range. Okay, emitting a steady stream of high-frequency sounds that vibrated her eardrums and gave a whole new meaning to the word "noise."

Just as Laura was thinking about distracting him with the toy rattle she held, Tucker's head popped up. He got quiet. Serious. And stared straight ahead, as if his baby radar had picked something up. He jerked his gaze to his left, toward the people fighting their way through the blinding snow on the crowded sidewalk. Laura's heart leaped into her throat. Was this kid the world's most unusual baby, or what? She bent to look in the same direction Tucker did. She saw nothing unusual.

"What is it? What's going on?" Grant asked.

Laura sat back, gazing at Grant's questioning expression. She exhaled and quietly said, "Look at Tucker. He's—" she felt silly even saying it "—I don't know…seen something? Heard something?"

"He has?" Grant asked, glancing at the baby. "Whoa. He certainly has." Grant captured one of the baby's fat little mitten-covered hands in his. "What is it, big guy?" Tucker didn't respond. Grant turned a sober expression to Laura. "Sometimes it's like he's not a kid, you know? I feel like he's way over my head, as if he's trying to communicate something to me and I'm not smart enough to catch on. Like Lassie. Remember? 'What is it, girl? Where's Timmy? Is he in the well…again?'"

"I know. I feel the same way." Laura leaned forward, peering past Grant to the crowds bustling by. "But what do you make of it? It's like he knows. I can't even begin to— Oh, my God. It's Ms. Gibson." Her heart pounding, her eyes wide, Laura clutched Grant's sleeve. "It's Ms. Gibson. He knew she'd come by— No, wait. He couldn't have known. But it's her. The caseworker, Grant. It's her, I swear it.''

"You're kidding. Where? Which one?"

"Her," Laura all but screeched, pointing out the window. "The African-American lady there. She has a briefcase. See? That's her. With the scarf. Hurry. Something's happened. Roll the window down."

Grant did as ordered. Instantly the cold and the noise of the city, the traffic, the honking, the policemen's whistles, the car tires rolling through slush assailed their ears. Tucker remained on point. Laura held onto him and leaned over Grant, calling out, "Ms. Gibson? Ms. Gibson? Here! In the cab. It's me—Laura Sloan. Over here."

Linda Gibson stopped and looked around. A pedestrian or two bumped into her, before she noticed the idling cab. Laura waved, held Tucker up...and recognition dawned in Ms. Gibson's eyes. She shouldered her way over, holding her coat closed against the wind that threatened to whisk her away. At the cab's side, she bent over to peer into the window and steadied herself with a hand on the door frame. "Ms. Sloan. Hello. Well, I see you have the—"

Her gaze lit on Grant. And froze. "Baby," she finally said. Her expression slowly changed. "I don't believe it. You weren't kidding. Wait until I tell—" She addressed Grant. "Do you know who you are? You're Grant Maguire."

"That's what I'm told, Ms. Gibson," Grant responded, offering a wide, sexy grin. "I'm pleased to meet you."

Show-off. Laura broke into the little adoring scene. "I didn't expect to see you out here. Has something happened?" No response. The woman still stared at Grant. "Ms. Gibson? Yoo-hoo?"

Ms. Gibson started and glanced Laura's way. Finally. But when she did, there was a new respect shining in her eyes. No, not respect. Speculation. Of the what sort of woman are you to get a man like this variety. Laura had seen the look before, when she and Grant were dating in college. She'd dismissed it then and she dismissed it now. "I was asking you if something has happened."

"Well, yes, it has. Your mother has all the details, but I might as well tell you in person," Ms. Gibson said, dividing her gaze between Laura and Grant. "The short version is, after a cup of hot tea with your mother, I called in to my supervisor to let her in on what was happening. And she informed me that this baby—" she pointed to Tucker, who remained strangely quiet and focused "—isn't the one we were looking for."

"What?" Laura cried, along with Grant. And along with Tucker—who didn't say what, but did squeal and chortle and awkwardly clap his mittened hands together, somewhat reminiscent of a baby seal.

"That's right," Ms. Gibson said, nodding, looking as happy for this turn of events as the three in the cab so obviously were. "The lady's real baby had been out with his dad. A miscommunication between the couple, apparently. Your mother said she knew that because she's psychic. But anyway, the family's been reunited and they have already gone home. And that's what I'm doing now, too. Going home."

Knee-weakening relief coursed through Laura's veins. She slumped against the seat, and felt Grant next to her do the same. She hugged Tucker to her, holding him even tighter as Grant turned to her, sheltering her and the baby in his thankful embrace. "Oh, thank God," Laura intoned.

"I can only apologize for the continued confusion," Ms. Gibson offered. "And tell you that, though glitches do occur in the system, it generally works. And works well. But speaking of glitches—" she chuckled "—I could have told you earlier this wasn't the right baby if I hadn't been so...well, put off balance by your mother. No offense meant."

"None taken," Laura laughingly assured her as she magnanimously forgave and embraced the entire world in her moment of euphoria. "She has that effect on everyone. But what do you mean, you could have told us earlier?"

"Well, if I'd thought to have you describe him, I could have saved you this trip. See, the baby we were looking for is Asian. And this little guy—" she grinned in Tucker's direction. Laura glanced down. Tucker was grinning right back "—is obviously not. But things being what they were with your report, and no description noted—again, not your fault—well, it was a shot in the dark, essentially. We had to check it out. I'm very sorry."

Laura nodded agreeably, then had a suddenly sobering thought. She didn't want to ask, but knew she had to. It was only right. "Did you say that you're on your way home?"

Ms. Gibson met her gaze and apparently picked up on the direction Laura's thoughts were taking. "Yes, I did. And listen, I don't know what to tell you about this little man. With the power out, the computers down and the phone lines going dead... Well—and I may get myself fired for even suggesting it—can you keep this baby with you until things clear up some?"

Stunned into happy speechlessness, Laura watched as Ms. Gibson looked from her to Grant and back. "Look," she said, "I'm satisfied he's safe and in good hands. And better off with you right now than he would be in custody, given the mess the whole city's in tonight. I'd just hate for such a little guy to fall through the cracks, you know what I mean? Is it too big of a problem for you to keep him for now?"

"A problem?" Grant beat Laura to the punch. But that was okay, because she was still too heart-stoppingly ecstatic to speak. "No problem at all. In fact, Ms. Gibson, I could kiss you for suggesting it." Ms. Gibson's jaw dropped. Laura grinned. "Of course, we'll keep him," Grant continued. "And for as long as necessary."

Then Grant covered the caseworker's hand with his. "And by the way, if you get fired for making such a humane decision, please let me know. I'll see to it that you don't have to hunt for a job."

He pulled back, looking the woman over. "In fact, fired or not, do you have a business card so we can reach you if something comes up?"

AT LEAST THE power's back on. Although God alone knows for how long, Grant thought as warm air whooshed comfortingly from the floor vents. He'd talked to his parents, giving them Laura's number, although he hoped they wouldn't use it. They'd gotten Tucker to sleep in his pillow-stuffed drawer. Feeling exhausted, Grant ambled down the three steps leading from Laura's bedroom in time to witness a mother-daughter exchange.

Somehow, seeing them there, so easy with each other, so close, so caring...well, hell, it just warmed his heart.

Instead of feeling left out, the sight of them together made him want to be included. To be one with Laura, to be a part of her crazy patchwork quilt of a family.

He grinned, a warm smile that mirrored his feelings toward the blond woman his gaze naturally sought and lingered on. He wondered if she knew what her nearness did to him. How her scent quickened his blood, how the sound of her voice changed his breathing. He ached to hold her, to touch her, to kiss his way down her entire body and right back up. *Whew. Easy, Maguire. The woman's mother is in the room.*

Grant tried to cool his thoughts. If Laura didn't know how he felt, whose fault was that? He shook his head, mentally scrolling through the problems and complications in his life. And came to one conclusion. It was time to act. Time to remedy a lot of situations.

But for now, he decided, coming back to the moment…well, there they were, two of the women he loved best in the whole world. He may as well enjoy them. Seated at opposite ends of the sofa, mother and daughter—could they be more different to be so closely related?—faced each other, talking. So at ease with each other. He approached quietly, grinning as he picked up the thread of their conversation.

"I *am* trying to tell you what took us so long to get back here, Mother. But you keep interrupting me."

"So, who's interrupting? Go ahead," Vivian interrupted.

Laura let out a sigh and tucked her legs under her. "So *then*," she said pointedly, "Grant gets her business card—"

"For what?"

Laura gestured with her hands. "So we can reach her if we need her, I guess."

Vivian leaned forward. "So why would you need her? I'm here now. That means the baby's safe."

Laura was silent. Then she said, "Thanks, Mother. You know, the Spanish Inquisition could have used your interrogation skills."

"Don't get smart with me, young lady. So where does this Miss Gibson live?"

"Where does she— How would I know? You're the psychic. You tell me."

Vivian pursed her lips. "Don't get fresh with me. You could learn a lot from that nice Miss Gibson. *She* didn't mind telling your stepfather I'm psychic."

"Telling my— How'd she do that, Mother? Irving left here before I went to work. And long before Ms. Gibson ever showed up."

"That he did. But just before she found out that precious little angel Tucker was the wrong baby—I told her all along he was, too—Irving called to say he was home with Esther, that all was well." She preened, shifting her weight, fluttering her fake eyelashes and arranging her fringed silk shawl around her shoulders. "Separated or not, he doesn't like for me to worry."

Laura chuckled and crossed her arms. "You're not separated, Mother."

Vivian sat up straighter. "He left me here. He's in Rhode Island. And I'm in New York. What would you call it?"

"A vacation. For Irving," Laura said wryly.

Vivian grimaced at her daughter. "And to think I carried you in my body for nine months to have you talk this way to me."

Laura laughed, reaching out to squeeze her mother's arm. "I'm sorry. Go on."

"Thank you," Vivian responded, with a condescend-

ing wave of her hand. "Well, anyway, when that nice
Miss Gibson found out what I'd been saying all along—
about the baby being the wrong one—was right, I had
her call Irving back and tell him as much. So there."
A very royal sniff preceded her next words. "I'll pay
for the call."

Grant saw Laura's shoulders hunch. No doubt, she
was cringing at the thought of poor Ms. Gibson alone
here, at Vivian's tender mercies. "I don't care about the
call. You don't have to pay for it. But wait a minute.
You had *her* call Irving, Mother?"

Vivian tsked, waving a dismissive hand at her eldest
child. "Why would I have her call him Mother? I had
her call him Mr. Pender— Oh."

"Oh is right, Mrs. *Smith.*" Laura laughed, leaning
forward to hug her mother fiercely. "Caught yourself
in your own little web of lies, didn't you?"

Although he hated like hell having to spoil their fun,
Grant put an index finger to his lips and made a hushing
sound. Obviously startled, Laura released her mother
and turned to him. Grant gestured with his thumb, indicating Sleeping Baby on Premises. Laura clapped a
hand over her mouth and drew her knees to her chest.
Grant winked at her and nonchalantly flopped down on
the sofa between Laura and Vivian, the latter of whom
patted his arm affectionately.

Grant winked at the older woman and turned to
Laura. "Whoever wakes that gripy little bear cub has
to deal with him. I got him to sleep, and I'm now officially off duty."

"Then," Vivian announced, hefting her rounded
body from the sofa, "that means I'm officially on
duty."

Laura lurched forward. "Mom, you don't have to do that. I know you're tired and I—"

"No, no, no," Vivian countered, dismissing Laura's protests with a wave of her heavily bejeweled hand. "I want to do this. I've waited a long time to have a grandchild, and I'm not— What's wrong with you?"

And well she should ask. Laura had collapsed dramatically across Grant's chest. Facedown. Grant chuckled, solicitously patting her slender back and feeling hot and heavy everywhere she touched him. If she didn't get up soon—

Laura abruptly sat. "No. Do not call him your grandson. Big no-no, Mother. Don't get attached. He's not ours." She glanced at Grant. He only offered a grin. Laura blinked, then swung her gaze to her mother. "I mean mine. No—yours. He's not your grandchild."

"We'll see," Vivian sang, picking up her suitcase from beside the overstuffed chair and heading for the steps that would take her up to Laura's bed. "I'll just sleep up here in case my little sweetie wakes up. Good night, all. You two kids get to bed soon, okay?"

On the sofa, the aforementioned "all" remained quiet, staring after her until she disappeared into the night-light-brightened darkness that encompassed Laura's bedroom. After another wordless moment, in which Vivian's parting statement about the two of them getting to bed hung almost tangibly in the air between them, Grant rubbed his hand over Laura's thigh, eliciting a hissing intake of breath from her. Which told him plainly enough that she'd been picturing that very thing. The two of them in bed. Together.

His heart thumping, he managed a sober expression. "You gotta like that woman. She's full of great ideas."

"Yes. She is, at that," Laura said, finally turning to

him to reveal gray eyes resembling silvered moonlight, the desire in them a sparkling reflection of Grant's own need.

His breath caught. "If you keep looking at me like that, Laura," he warned, "we're going to—"

Her hand slid up his thigh, her mouth curving into a seductive grin. "End up in bed together?" She wet her lips with her tongue and added, "Soon, I hope."

Grant's mouth opened. But no words came out. Finally, in a husky voice, he asked, "Oh, baby, are you sure?"

"That I want you? Yes, I'm sure. Am I sure that we should do this?" A quick grin, one of some uncertainty, flashed across her delicately feminine features. "No, I'm not sure. But...I can't seem to help myself, Grant."

"I know what you mean. And I know I should stay away from you."

She cocked her head at a questioning angle. "Why do you know that?"

These looks she was giving him. He couldn't think straight. "Because I...walked out...ten years ago."

"We've talked about this. You were just a kid. We both were. We're all grown up now."

"I know. But we haven't said anything about...now. Or tomorrow. Or the next day. If we do this, everything will be different. Between us."

"Aren't I supposed to be the one worried about such things?" she teased.

But Grant was serious. "Yes. You should. That's the way this world works, it seems. But God knows, I've done everything I could to be near you this past month. That should tell you something."

"It does. But don't tell me you're going to give up

now?'' She gave another quick grin, then slid her hand farther up his thigh. "I like that you've pursued me.''

"Yeah? Then why'd you run?''

"I don't know,'' she said, shrugging as her gaze roved over his body. Grant's stomach muscles contracted. "I was just scared, I guess. Scared I'd feel this way. And you wouldn't. But I didn't run far.'' She met his gaze. "Or for long, did I?''

"No, you didn't.'' Amused, aroused, Grant shook his head slowly and slouched into the sofa. And it seemed like the most natural thing in the world for him to run his hand up under her sweater, caressing the warm, taut flesh that covered her rib cage.

She stiffened, arching her back. A tiny moan of pleasure escaped her. Grant's senses came alive. He'd done this a thousand times before, all those years ago. But now, tonight, ten years later, it was so much richer. And her skin still felt so inviting to his touch. Like hot silk. Emboldened by her response, he moved his hand up, found a bra-encased breast and caressed it gently. Her flesh was so full in his hand. So warm and heavy. Like a ripe fruit with a hard bud of desire in its middle.

"Grant,'' Laura whispered, raggedly. Her eyes closed, her breathing changed, became shallow, gasping, and her expression became more rapturous as Grant continued to stroke her budded nipple. "Please...''

He felt on the edge. Hard. Ready. And it was then, even though no words had passed between them, that Grant knew that tonight and for every night to follow, he wanted to see this look on her face. With that decision, he slid his hand from under her sweater and pulled her to him, lifting her with him, carrying her in his arms, across the loft toward the other bedrooms. He had the

sudden urge to try out that enticing sleigh bed he'd seen
only this morning.

GLISTENING with perspiration, splayed out naked on the
queen-size sleigh bed, hopelessly entangled in the
covers, Laura lay there, her eyes wide, her breathing
slowly returning to normal. Which really seemed like
such a waste, given the magnificence of her bed com-
panion. Who even now, more or less at her side,
sounded no better—or just as well-loved, maybe—as
she did.

"Damn...we're good at...that," Grant said between
labored breaths.

"We always were," Laura reminded him, turning
onto her side and snuggling against him, her head on
his shoulder. Content for the moment, she draped a leg
over his and smoothed a hand across his chest, reveling
in the feel of the tight, warm skin overlying hard muscle
and in the crisp ticklishness of his chest hair. Smiling
all the way to her toes, she murmured, "You feel so
good, Grant. I love everything about you."

Then Laura froze. Her eyes, which had drifted shut,
popped open, and she felt cold all over. She'd said the
L-word. It hung over them like a jagged icicle, drip-
drip-dripping its truth on them. Holding her breath, she
stared at her hand on Grant's chest. And refused to think
about his sudden stillness. They'd not spoken of love,
of staying together, of commitment to one another. So
why had she said it? Maybe because she felt it? Because
it was true? And shouldn't that be what was important?
In a perfect world, maybe. But not this one.

Still, she refused to accept that, lying next to Grant
and feeling his chest rise and fall under her hand with
each breath he took. Come on, wasn't that where they

were headed, toward love? Surely it was. Look where they were and what they'd been doing...and doing. She remained silent. She'd said enough already, in her estimation. But my, weren't those wordless seconds really stretching out? Yes. Frighteningly, achingly so, actually.

Then, slowly enough for Laura's heart to rush through three or four more beats, Grant turned his head and stared into her eyes, his amber ones seeming to search hers for something. For what, she didn't know. Evidence of love? Or perhaps it was sanity he searched for. Sanity regarding their situation, their separate lives, their differing worlds. Who knew? Well, he did. So it was his turn to speak.

Or to turn more fully to her, to cover her body with his and kiss her deeply. Which was what he did, all without one word passing between them.

Laura barely noticed as once more she experienced the slow, sizzling slide of his skin over hers, as once more she reveled in their differences, his hardness against her softness, his leanness against her fullness, his firmness against her gentleness. As once more she delighted in the tastes, the scents, the sweet saltiness of his skin, the heady wine of his penetrating kiss, the devastating tenderness of his touch, its underlying current of passion held in check, of power leashed so as not to frighten.

As Grant moved lower on her, his hands and his mouth slowly playing her yearning body like a fine violin, as the heat once again built, Laura knew she could not have asked for more in a lover. But this was Grant, not just any mere lover. This man was meant to touch her. She'd been made for him. And he'd been made for her. Laura squeezed his shoulders with both hands. "Oh, Grant, I've needed you so."

"Me, too, baby," he murmured seductively while nipping kisses across her belly. "Since the moment—" he slowly swirled his tongue around her navel, dipping into it "—I first saw you—" he moved lower, cupping her buttocks in his hands "—over ten years ago."

And then his head went lower, raising her to his mouth. Suddenly, with a gasping intake of breath, Laura knew there would be no more words...only sensations, feelings, urges driven to the brink, passion coiled into a tight, hot bud that all too soon had her arching her back, gripping the sheets and making noises she'd never made before in her life.

Grant was relentless, sighing, making some of the same noises, drinking her in, enjoying her, loving her. She could feel it, could feel his heat, his grip tightening on her wetness, her female bud engorging, cresting...until it happened. She called his name all the way from the bottom of her soul as he took her with him over the edge, into the abyss, into the dark fires of urges gratified, of yearnings slaked.

For wonderfully agonizing seconds, Laura hovered there, quivering, every muscle locked, her entire being honed in on the delicious spasms that rocked her body, that undulated outward from her core, that burned through her soul like licking flames.

And then, when she could take no more, Grant pulled himself up, kissing his way up her, swirling his tongue over her nipples, suckling her. He raised up over her, bracing himself. She drew her legs up and apart, and he entered her, sheathing himself in her. And she sighed with the sheer pleasure of it all as she wrapped her legs around his hips. For the third time that night.

But for the first of many nights Laura hoped would come.

8

LAURA STARED indulgently at Grant across the breakfast table. He was essentially ignoring her, but companionably so, as he devoured not only the morning newspaper—how *do* those delivery people get through, anyway, on a day when everything else is snowed under?—but also the huge breakfast her mother had prepared for them.

There was no sense letting all that electricity and this good food go to waste, Vivian had declared. There was no telling when it might go off again and they'd all starve to death, if they didn't freeze first. *As if.* Laura chuckled, pulling her thoughts to the guys across the table from her. That's right. Guys.

Because Grant, to further imitate this Norman Rockwell scene of American family life, was holding Tucker in his lap and commenting to the diaper-changed and cereal-fed baby about the various items he read, asking the tyke's opinion on world issues. Laura knew that neither he nor she would have been the least bit surprised if Tucker suddenly rendered a considered opinion. But whatever he thought, he kept it to himself, seemingly content to bang on the round table with a wooden spoon.

Laura chuckled softly. Quite the domestic picture, this. Here she was, in her gown and robe and thick socks, sipping coffee, ignoring her housecoated mother's still-at-the-stove-and-cooking pleas to her to eat more. When only last evening she'd asked Laura if she was gaining weight.

Mothers. There was no pleasing them, came Laura's indulgent thought. Her gaze moved from Grant to the scene outside. It looked like what you'd expect to see in some Old Master's painted depiction of Creation. Roiling gray clouds. Swirling winds. Chilling cold. Fourteen thousand tons of falling snow.

All it lacked was a muscled arm and a questing hand coming out of the clouds, reaching for Man. Laura's gaze slid to Grant. There was one man she wouldn't mind reaching for, herself. Again and again. Grant suddenly looked at her, as if he'd felt the weight of her stare. He winked slowly, seductively. Laura bit her bottom lip hard to keep from giggling and drawing her mother's attention their silly, lovesick way. Quite maturely, she again cast her gaze on the world outside her window.

The raging snowstorm showed no signs of letting up. Twice during the night, the power had gone out, and the three of them—Laura, Grant and Vivian—had been up, checking on the baby, preparing the centrally located fireplace in case it got too cold. But through it all, the pointless getting up and the going back to bed—as if a power outage required them to do so—there was that one moment, somewhere deep in the night that Laura would never forget. It clung to the corners of her thoughts, like dust motes in an attic, making her wonder. Had she heard him? Had he actually said it?

She couldn't be sure, but she thought, just before she'd dropped off to sleep, that she'd heard Grant whisper into her ear, "I love you, too, Laura."

Or did she just want it to be true? Well, he'd certainly

acted like it last night. Okay, so had she. And, boy, was she proud of her own performance, too. She'd made that man more than moan. She'd left him weak-kneed and hanging on to the bed when he tried to stand. In fact, for a while there, he'd been unable to articulate words containing vowels.

Laura grinned, a private, leering grin she hid behind her raised coffee mug. *Damn, I'm good,* she congratulated herself. But she had to admit that it was because of Grant. Because she'd been with him. Because she'd wanted to give so much of herself to him. She'd wanted him, needed him...loved him. And now, no matter what happened today, at least, she had last night. It was a private, treasured gift she'd given herself, one she could take out from its hiding place in her heart and play with when she was alone. If she was alone. Again.

"Pssst, Laura."

Laura blinked, sat her mug down and stared at Grant. He was leaning over the table, the baby still perched on one of his knees. She frowned. *What?*

Grant spared a glance her mother's way. Tucker did the same. Laura followed suit. Vivian had her back to them. Laura swung her gaze to Grant. And to Tucker. Both of whom stared at her. Grant put his hands over the baby's ears. Tucker's sudden frown said he was insulted. "I can actually see what you're thinking," Grant whispered. "It's written all over your face. Shame on you."

A flush of embarrassed heat rose in Laura's cheeks. But despite it, she grinned wickedly at him. Leaning over the table toward him, she whispered, "That's not what you said last night."

He chuckled, undressing her with his eyes. She was enjoying it until a voice called out, over the banging pots and pans, "I'm not deaf, you know. I can hear you. Just like I heard you last night. All three times. And I ask you, is this any way to talk with a baby in the room?"

Laura sucked in her breath, jerking back and staring wide-eyed at Grant.

"I just hope you two used some protection. You know, all that safe-sex stuff you hear so much about."

"Mother!" Laura cried, her cheeks ablaze with a crimson heat. Grant laughed out loud and sat the baby on the table, facing him. Tucker rewarded him by knighting him with his wooden spoon. Bonk, right on the end of Grant's nose. "Ouch," Grant yelped, rubbing his nose with one hand and steadying Tucker with the other. "All right, you win. What a tough crowd." He turned to Vivian. "We used protection, Vivian."

"Every time?"

Laura buried her face in her hands and heard Grant's laugh. "Every time. I swear."

"Yeah? Where'd you get the condoms?"

Laura jerked her head up. She couldn't believe this! "Will you look who's preaching safe sex? I mean, can we talk about Esther? Just accept, Mother, that *responsible* adults either carry protection with them or keep a supply on hand. Just in case."

Vivian turned ever so slowly, a grease-dripping spatula in her bejeweled hand. "Am I hearing you right? *You,* my first baby, keep a supply on hand?"

Thoroughly embarrassed, particularly because Grant was laughing his head off, Laura answered, "I'm thirty years old, Mother. But I really don't want to talk about it. Not with you. Please."

"Fine," Vivian huffed. "But you leave your baby sister out of this. She was conceived in love. Not lust.

But I'm not happy about this supply of yours." She sighed. "Well, I'm glad you're taking precautions for your health and all. Don't believe everything you see on those commercials."

She couldn't help herself. Laura took the bait. "What commercials, Mother?"

"You know. The ones with the movie stars telling us— Ha! Like they're so healthy. Forget TV. Pick up a newspaper, for God's sake. Read it for yourself."

Laura took a deep breath. "What commercials, Mother?"

Vivian gestured at her with the spatula. "You know the ones. Where the movie stars tell us to use condoms, so we can— What does that guy with the pointy ears say?"

Every individual strand of hair on Laura's head ached. Before she could stop Grant—she could only conclude that he must be out of practice after a ten-year absence—he asked, "Pointy ears? You mean like a werewolf?"

Knowing what the poor slob was in for, Laura put her elbow on the table and rested her aching head in it.

"No. That's in real life," Vivian said. "I mean on TV. In the future. You know. Oh, yeah. 'Live long and prosper.' That man. The one who can kill you with a pinch. That's what the movie stars want."

"They want to kill us with a pinch?" Apparently, Grant hadn't learned his lesson yet.

Vivian huffed. "No, Grant. That was just a euphemism. A synonym, I mean. What I'm trying to say is, they want *us* to live long and buy movie tickets so *they* can prosper. See what I mean?"

Laura jumped at the opening given her. "Mother,

since I *met* you, I haven't known what you've meant. So how can Grant hope to—''

Vivian waved her hand, cutting off Laura and otherwise ignoring her as she continued. "So who are they kidding, anyway, Grant? They don't use condoms. Or there wouldn't be so many of them. Movie stars, I mean. But my point is, if you two keep using birth control, how's Tucker ever going to have a baby sister?''

Laura froze. *That* was her point? The ensuing and weighty silence was enough to melt Laura's fillings. She peered at Grant through her splayed fingers. Sure enough, the man looked shell-shocked. Laura could not believe this conversation. And the worst part of it was that this open, healthy and frank discussion was about *her* sex life. With her lover, her mother and a baby present. Over breakfast. It was enough to put her on a psychiatrist's couch for the next fifteen years.

The electricity blinked off. Lights. Radio. Heat. Stove. Refrigerator. Off. Vivian squawked. Tucker screeched. Grant soothed. And Laura slumped in relief. *Oh, thank you, kind snowstorm of the century, for hearing my plea.*

Well, not quite, apparently, because the electricity came right back on. Warm air rushed through the vents. The track lighting, suspended from the high and raftered ceiling, flicked to life. The bacon in the frying pan sizzled. And so did Vivian. "Don't *you* think Tucker needs a baby sister, Grant?'' she persisted, as if there'd been no break in their conversation.

Laura stole a look at Grant. The grim set of his mouth told its own story as he gently reminded Vivian, "He may already have one, for all we know, Viv. He's not ours, remember.''

Vivian's chin suddenly trembled. Her eyes grew moist. "I know that. He's just such a sweet little—" She turned abruptly.

Her heart melting, Laura instantly forgave her mother for bringing up such a sore subject. Poor sweet Viv. There was nothing she loved more than a baby. And Laura wanted nothing more than to go to her mother and put an arm around her. But she wasn't sure her legs would carry her. Because sitting there talking about babies brought the situation home again. She looked at Tucker and wondered when the knock on the door would come. What would they all do?

Vivian turned, her eyes dry, her mouth set with stubbornness. "Well, he can't already have a baby sister. So there. He's just a baby himself. And it doesn't take a rocket surgeon or a brain scientist to know his mother couldn't have had another one yet. Ha. Now you come here and finish frying this bacon, Laura. And Grant, give me that baby."

Laura stared at her mother as, her arms extended, her long-nailed hands poised to take the baby, she advanced on Grant and Tucker. Laura swung her gaze to Grant, who mouthed, *Rocket surgeon?* Right back at him, Laura mouthed, *Brain scientist?* They both shrugged.

After Grant spinelessly handed the baby to Vivian, she admonished, "Grant, you haven't called your parents this morning. They'll be worried. So you do that. And in the meanwhile, I'll go get the baby's stuff together. No, wait. First you two eat that bacon and then clean up this mess. Be sure to get that sink good and clean." She turned to Laura, singling her out. "Because you're going to give him a bath in it."

"Me? I'm going to? In the sink?" Laura heard herself echoing.

"Trust me," Grant said, capturing Laura's attention, "the sink makes perfect sense. Ask Tucker about our shower here yesterday morning."

Vivian honed in on Grant like a bird dog on point. "You were the company here yesterday? That's it. When can I expect to see a ring on my child's finger, young man?"

"Mother!" Laura warned.

"Oh, fine then. Live in sin." To Tucker, she cooed, "Come on, sweetie. That's right. Grandma's got you now. What do you think of that, huh?"

The frantic expression on Tucker's face quite plainly, yet eloquently showed his opinion. He held his arms out straight over Vivian's shoulder wagging his chubby little hands, begging for Laura and Grant, as if to say, *I'll give you a thousand dollars to rescue me from this scary woman.*

"EXCUSE ME. Weren't you the one who said this would be easier?"

"Yeah, well, I lied," Grant snapped as he reached again for a slippery, soapy baby arm and tried to hold Tucker's bouncing little body steady in the cream-colored enamel kitchen sink.

At Grant's side, Laura measured yet another portion of baby shampoo into her palm. "Sit him down before he falls," she warned.

"Tell *him* that," Grant groused, his voice strained with his efforts. But apparently Tucker preferred trying repeatedly to stand, thereby showing the world his naked goods, over sitting sedately in the warm water and being modest. And cooperative. Well, okay, not that there was much water left in the sink for him to sit in.

Laura cupped the amber-colored shampoo blob in her

hand. "Grant, I'm serious. You need to get him to sit down."

The baby arm and its owner got away from Grant. He reached two-handed for a submarine-diving chubby torso, got a good grip and turned to Laura. "Doesn't it look like I'm trying here? Maybe some superglue—"

"That's not funny." Laura fussed, swiping her sopping arm under her nose, which allowed the shampoo to run out of her hand and onto the already inundated floor. She stared at the blob it made. "Aw, man. That's the third time I did that. Son of a—"

"Uh-uh," Grant warned, nodding toward the baby. "Mr. Radar Ears repeats everything he hears. Ask me how I know."

"I think I can guess." Laura braced her hands on the sink's edge, her expression falling. "Grant, why is this so hard for me? I mean the baby. Everything about him. And kids in general. Why can't I do anything right with them? Look at you. You caught on just fine."

"Well, I don't know about just fine. I nearly drowned him in the shower yesterday and got a diaper tab stuck to his skin." He looked at the laughing baby. "Oh, yeah, I also taught him how to cuss."

"You know what I mean."

He nodded. "Yeah, I do. But I don't see that you're doing anything wrong, Laura. Come on, no one expects you to catch on right away. Give yourself a chance. It'll come to you. Just relax. And look at Tucker. He's fine—despite our best efforts." Grant grinned, nodding toward Tucker, who splashed with chubby, stiff-armed movements at the remaining water in the sink and peered bright-eyed at them, screeching his happiness. Grant chuckled. "See?"

She grinned—how could she not in the face of such

cuteness?—but it didn't seem to make her feel any better. "Yeah, I see. But if he's fine, it's because you and my mother are here. I'm serious. I couldn't do this by myself. I'd probably pull the plug on this sink and he'd go down the drain with the water. How would I explain that? And you heard my mother last night. My own flesh and blood. She said Tucker's *safe* now because she's here."

Grant looked at her for a moment, then quietly asked, "Laura, what's really wrong here?"

Her expression crumpling, she sniffed and avoided his gaze. "How am I ever going to be a mother, Grant? My own kids won't be safe with me."

Aha. But even in the face of such demoralization—and because he truly believed she would be a wonderful mother—Grant couldn't resist throwing her own words at her. "You said you weren't going to have kids. No marriage. No kids. Remember?"

Laura's expression firmed. She narrowed her eyes at him. "I remember."

Grant chuckled. "So what's different now? Don't tell me forever is already here."

She grinned. She didn't want to, he could tell, but she did grin. "Didn't you read about it in the newspaper? The front-page headline read, Pigs Fly out of a Frozen Hell. That loosely translates to Forever Has Arrived."

Grant laughed at her. It wasn't hard. She was so damned funny. And endearing. And dressed like some football team's deranged version of a cowgirl cheerleader. In jeans and a sweatshirt, her straight hair ponytailed, a huge bath towel pinned around her neck like a bandanna. She'd said it would keep her clothes dry. It hadn't. "All right, so forever is here. Does that mean you now want to get married and have kids of your own?''

Her eyes widened. Grant looked at Tucker. His blue eyes were also wide.

Laura answered, "I might. Why? Are you…are you asking?''

Was he? Grant didn't know what to say. He exchanged another look with Tucker, who was suddenly very attentive. And still. Always a sign of something important. Grant frowned, wondering why he didn't feel cornered by her question. Shouldn't he? He'd always felt that way before. But not now. "I just did…ask you…in the general sense,'' he hedged—noncommittally, until he could think this through.

"Oh,'' Laura responded. "Then, um, yes. In the general sense. I'd like to get married and have kids. Some day. With someone.''

Some day? With someone? Maintaining his hold on the baby, Grant grinned, wanting to kiss her all over. "That's good to hear. I wish you a lot of luck with that.''

Her eyes narrowed. "Thanks. I'll send you an invitation.''

"I'd like that.''

A wordless moment passed. "You are not helping.''

Grant grinned. "You're right. Time to get serious before Tucker here turns into a Popsicle.'' Grant fisted a wet and soapy hand and raised it. "Come on, Laura. Once more with feeling. We can do this. You're bigger than he is. He's just one little baby.''

She and Tucker eyed him as if he'd taken leave of his senses. Clearly, they remained unconvinced. "One little baby?'' Laura chided. "Grant, once, when I was little—'' she picked up the shampoo bottle and measured another portion into her palm "— we took a family vacation to Florida and saw this guy there who made a living wrestling live alligators."

"Yeah? So?" Grant looked up from holding onto the happily splashing Tucker to glance at Laura. "What's that got to do with—"

"I'll tell you. That old man had less trouble doing that—all by himself—than we...the two of us...are having here. With one *little* baby. And that alligator was not little, Grant. It must've weighed eight or nine hundred pounds. That's all I'm saying." With that, she plopped the shampoo dollop onto Tucker's head and earned the same frowning, nose-wrinkled-up face he gave when she told him no.

Grant held onto the child for dear life as Laura scrubbed away. But still, he felt compelled to argue, although perhaps not wisely at this point. "Oh, come on, eight or nine hundred pounds? I doubt it. But still, even if it was...the alligator, I mean...do you really think the guy was as good at wrestling him the first time he did it as he was the day you saw him?"

Laura stopped scrubbing Tucker's head, braced her soapy hands on the sink's edges and turned to him. "Yeah, I do. Don't you think he'd have to be, Grant? After all, if he hadn't been somewhat competent from the get-go, he'd have been gator kibble that first time out. Right?"

It was frightening, how much she looked and sounded like her mother. "I guess," Grant finally conceded, although he wasn't certain what he was conceding to exactly. But apparently he'd goofed. Laura continued to stare in silence at him. So did Tucker, whose soapy cap of lather had began running down his forehead and neck. Feeling under the gun, Grant ventured, "Maybe you're right. I guess it's like those cliff divers in Mexico. I mean, how do they know they're good at that until the first time they jump, huh?''

Laura shook her head. "Fine. Don't answer me."

"But I did," Grant protested, feeling very much like a domesticated male at the moment. A clueless, therefore successful, domesticated male. "I answered you."

"Oh, as if we were really talking about cliff divers and alligators, Grant."

"We weren't?" It was news to him.

"Hardly," Laura assured him, turning to the blinking baby just in time to swipe a shampoo bubble out of his eyes and save them from having to test the no-more-tears claim. "We were talking about suitability to a task. And the task here was parenting."

Again, it was news to Grant. "It was?"

"Yes. It was." She looked really sad about that. As if they'd failed. She issued more instructions. "Oh, forget it. Just hold him back. No, the other way. Like Mom said. Like at a beauty shop. There. Like that. No. Wait. Sit him up. We need more water. Can you— No, just hold him. Let me—" she moved the spout to the other basin and turned the water on. "Okay, it's almost warm enough—"

The intercom buzzed.

Laura lost it. "Oh, for Pete's sake, *now* what?" Then she yelled, "Mom? Are you in the tub yet?"

They waited. Silence. Then a singsong voice called back, "No. I was getting my towel. Why?"

"The intercom just buzzed. Can you answer it?"

"Okay. Just a minute, though. Let me get my robe."

"Thanks," Laura called. She glanced at Grant, noticing his crestfallen expression. "What?"

Grant shrugged. "Nothing. Just wondering who that might be. On a day like this. That's all."

"Oh," she said, sniffing and turning to the running water, putting her finger under the stream to test its temperature. It looked as if she'd just understood what the buzzer could mean. A sad little frown settled on her face. "It could be anybody."

"Yeah. It could," he agreed. But he knew better, and suspected she did, too. After all, they weren't at work because the entire city had been shut down. The weather wasn't expected to clear until sometime this afternoon. And then they'd have to dig themselves out. So... friends? Not likely. Delivery man? Doubtful.

But still, seeing Laura unhappy ate at Grant. It gnawed him inside out. He had tons of money and yet he couldn't put a smile on her face. *Dammit.* He clenched his jaw. He wanted to...well, he didn't know what. So he let out his breath and bent over, bracing his elbows on the sink's edge, keeping his grip on the suddenly still Tucker. With only the sound of the running water filling the room, they waited.

The silence was broken by Vivian, calling loudly through the intercom, as if she needed to yell her message downstairs. "Hello? Who? Hawkins? Officer Hawkins? Ooh, wait...I'm getting something. My psychic powers are— You're a policeman, right? Yes? Ha! I knew you were." Pause. "Yes, I did." Pause. "Yes, I did." Then, "So, how can I— Huh? Okay, hold on. Let me see."

Then, in a stage whisper so loud they heard it in the kitchen, Vivian called, "Laura? It's an Officer Hawkins. He wants to know if you're here. What should I tell him?"

Frozen in place at the mention of Officer Hawkins—

the policeman who thought *their* baby was missing—
Grant and Laura exchanged a look. Grant couldn't think
what to do fast enough. But apparently Laura could.
"Does she really think he will believe that she doesn't
know if I'm here or not?" she asked Grant. Then in a
louder voice, she said, "He just heard you talking to
me, Mother, if you're still holding the button down."

"Oops."

Grant shook his head. Laura did, too. "What else can
we do?" she said rhetorically. "Buzz him up, Mother."
Then, together, silently, they listened as Vivian did just
that. "Mother? Did you let go of the button yet?"

"Yes—no. Okay, yes, I did just now."

Laura shook her head in a long-suffering way.
"Good. Stay there. And listen to me. When he comes
up, keep him by the doors and don't let him know that
Tucker is here. He thinks Grant and I are married and
that our baby is missing. Don't tell him otherwise,
okay? Let's just see what he wants."

A heavy silence ensued. Then, from the front door,
Vivian called, "I like that story. Well, except about the
missing baby. But...okay."

Laura exhaled in relief and looked at Grant. "She
can do it. She's a great liar. When the cause is right."

Despite everything, Grant chuckled. "That's nice to
know." He sobered. "This will be okay, Laura. We'll
get through it. And we'll be fine."

She stared at him. "We? Is there a we, Grant? And
what about Tucker? How do I—do we—just let him
go? I mean, *can* you? Because I don't think I can. Even
though he's not mine. And even though I'm probably
putting his life at risk. After Tucker will there be a we,
a me and a you? I don't know."

Her worries silenced Grant. His arms braced against

the counter, he swallowed around the sudden lump in his throat and hung his head. Then he looked at Tucker. Who winked at him.

Surprised, Grant raised his eyebrows. He pulled back, not trusting what he'd seen. Surely the baby had just blinked. Not winked, but blinked. Babies do that all the time. *With one eye?* Grant's belly tensed. "What is it, buddy? You know something, don't you?"

"What did you say?" Laura asked.

Grant looked at where she stood next to him. "He knows something. Look at him."

Laura looked, and her eyes widened. She turned to Grant. "He just winked at me. Did you see that?"

Grant grinned. "Yeah. He did the same to me. Just now."

"He did? Wait a minute. I remember him doing this before, Grant." Excited, she began hitting his arm. Watery suds flew with every smack. "When I first got him? He winked at me. Let's see. It was— Well, I forget. But something good happened after that. I remember that much."

Grant stared into her eyes and felt a grin forming on his face. Could he love her any more than he did right now? And then he knew he needed to tell her. Right now. Out loud. Before things got more complicated. So she'd know that no matter what happened with Tucker, he loved her. He was here for her. And he was staying. Last night he'd told her he loved her. But she hadn't answered him.

It had hurt. But here he was getting ready to say it again. What if she didn't say it back? Oh, to hell with the consequences. He felt it. And he was going to tell her. That he wanted to be the someone she married some day. He wanted to be the one she had babies with. "Laura," he said, "I want to—"

"Grant, wait," she said, cutting him off. He swallowed his words as she frantically whispered, "What are we doing? That policeman is at the front door. Hear him talking? We have got to get this baby's hair rinsed and get out of here—" she swung the spout and the running water to the sink in which Tucker sat, much to his interested delight "—or at least out of this room."

Caught up in her frantic activity, Grant quietly leaned Tucker back and began rinsing his hair. "But we don't even know what this guy wants, Laura."

"Which is exactly my point," she whispered. "If he doesn't know any different than he did before, we need to hide this baby. And if he does know Tucker's here—" She gasped, grabbing Grant's arm and squeezing hard. Her eyes were like saucers. "Dear God, what if there's some law against bathing babies in sinks? We—okay, you—have already lied to Officer Hawkins once..."

"Me?" It was hard to whisper when being accused. "Thanks. Give me up. I told you I couldn't get two words in—"

"Grant, is that important now? Just help me." With that, she reached for a baby towel, one with the sewn-in pocket for the baby's head. "Rinse his hair and then hand him to me."

But Grant wanted to speak his heart. "Hold on. I will. But first, I want to tell you, Laura, that I—"

"Grant, please. Let's deal with the baby first." She began quietly and quickly to gather the scattered evidence of the child's presence. Rubber ducky, baby shampoo, bottle cap, soiled outfit...

But Grant had an agenda, too—one he wanted to see

through. Holding Tucker with one hand, Grant grabbed Laura's arm with the other, holding her steady, capturing her startled attention. "No. It can't wait. Will you listen to me, please?"

Exasperated, she whispered, "All right. I'm listening."

Well, this wasn't the least bit romantic. "Not like this. I wanted it to be—"

Laura sucked in her breath and clutched him. And Grant knew why. Vivian's voice, along with the officer's, was getting louder. And not in a good way. The door slammed. Who'd left? Or had someone come in? Laura held Grant's sweatshirt with both wet and soapy hands. "I swear I will listen to you in a minute. I swear. Just—for now, okay, please help me get this baby— aw!"

So much for subterfuge. Grant jumped, watching in frozen horror as Laura was soaked from head to foot with the sink's spray hose. Held in Tucker's hands even as he, Grant, held one of the child's arms. It was a real fluke that Tucker could get a good grip on it. That's what it was. A fluke. It had to be. *Yeah, right.* Who was this kid? *What* was this kid?

"Grant!" Laura shrieked. "Do something! Get it away from him!" Trapped by the breakfast bar and the steady jet of water, she raised her hands, trying to fend off a soaking.

Suddenly remembering that he should be doing more than holding onto the perpetrator, Grant put his body in harm's way. He threw himself between Laura and the jet of water. And got soaked for his efforts. Vivian jumped into the fray. She grabbed Tucker as Grant grabbed the hose, kinking it in one hand while with the other he furiously worked the spigots, finally getting the water shut off.

And then, with a dripping Tucker in Vivian's arms as she wrapped her dry bath towel around him, they all stood there in their varying degrees of wetness. And stared at each other. Then they started laughing. In ripples and waves that seemed to build on each other.

Vivian, with Tucker firmly wrapped, plopped down on a bar stool with him. Laura slid down the kitchen wall, holding her stomach, laughing until she cried. Grant followed suit, sliding down the wood cabinets until he, too, sat in a pool of water and dollops of shampoo. His arms slung around his bent knees, he leaned his head to rest it against a cabinet door and gave in to the hilarity.

After a while, they all began to quiet. Laura asked, "Mother, where's Officer Hawkins?"

"Oh, that nice young man? He's gone."

"Gone?" Laura looked at Grant. He made a go-figure face at her. She grinned and turned to Vivian. "What did you say to him?"

"The truth."

"Dear God."

"No, not that truth. The one you told me to say. Well, I would've, anyway. But he didn't know anything about the baby. He was just letting you know that despite the snow, the situation is under control."

And that was even funnier. *Under control?* Again, they burst out laughing. A minute or so later, Laura said, "Grant?"

He turned his head, looking her way. She looked terrible. Hair flattened and streaming. Clothes soaked. That damned towel pinned to her like a huge bib. And yet beautiful. She looked beautiful, too. He grinned. "Yeah?"

"What in the world was so important that you had to say it right then?"

"Forget it," he told her. "I'm over it."

"No. Tell me. I want to hear."

Grant nodded. "All right. But just remember. You asked me."

With that, the room got quiet. Deathly—okay, curiously—so. *What the hell,* Grant decided. What did he care if Vivian heard it? She'd know sooner or later, anyway. He shrugged. "No big deal. I just wanted to tell you that I love you."

9

LAURA DIDN'T KNOW what to think. Perhaps because she couldn't. After all, a meteor had just been dropped on top of her. A big, fat, heavy meteor. From the outer reaches of the far-flung, uncharted heavens. With no advance warning. Okay, no real advance warning. Maybe a hint or two. But nothing more. And, boy, under these circumstances, did it ever make her mad. "You what?"

Looking very unsure of himself, much as if he'd just realized he blurted, at a gathering of the Daughters of the American Revolution, that, Uh-huh, George Washington was, too, a liar, Grant turned away from her, looking to Vivian and Tucker. For help? But he wasn't getting any reinforcement from that direction. Instead, they were... Laura swiped more water out of her eyes. Staring. With excitement? With happiness? Both?

So, why aren't I?

Well, maybe, she defended herself, it was because she was tired, defeated and soaked. And sitting in a pool of water with her hair streaming in her eyes, a bath towel pinned around her neck and her life falling apart in front of her eyes. And the electrical power. Who knew when that would— It went off again. *Well, I'll be damned.*

Taking the darkness as an omen, Laura asked, "You what?" She looked into Grant's amber eyes, willing him to answer before she lost her nerve. "What did you just say, Grant Leon Maguire?"

He shrugged. "You mean, I love you? That?"

Laura nodded. "Yeah, Grant. I meant that. What were you thinking?"

He shrugged. "That I love you?"

Laura crossed her arms over her sodden chest. "I could just pinch you."

"Why?"

She shifted, causing her bedraggled ponytail to flop over her shoulder and, smack soggily against her cheek. "Why? You ask *why?* Because, you ninny, I've dreamed about this moment—"

"You have? Does that mean you love me, too?"

She swiped the ponytail away. "Of course I do. But it wasn't supposed to be like this. I wanted candlelight and dinner and music, darn you." She pulled herself up, gesturing out imaginary scenes. "And I had on this long black dress, and my hair was up. And you were in a tuxedo. Or—or maybe I just saw you one day on the street. By chance. And our eyes met—"

"They did?"

"Yes. And you took one look at me and swept me up in your arms, saying you'd been wrong and you couldn't live another day without me—"

"I can't."

"I know. Or another time—"

"There were other times?"

"Yes. Another time I was in a bookstore and I moved this book aside on a really tall shelf and—"

"There I was. On the other side."

"Yeah. And there you were. On the other side. And you said, 'Laura!' Like you were glad to see me."

"I'm sure I was."

"You were. And we had coffee, and—"

"I hope not one of those fancy mochalatta frangipani things. I hate those."

"No. The real kind. Like you like. And we talked and talked—"

"About what?"

"I don't know. Stuff. Our lives, I guess. And about how successful we'd become." She stopped, wiping away the tears that streamed down her cheeks. "And about how empty our lives were—"

"Without each other?"

"Yeah. And—"

"That's what I'm trying to tell you now, Laura."

"I know. And—" Finally—*finally!*—she stopped herself. And heard him. Everything he'd said. She wiped her eyes, realizing she'd at some point come to her feet. And so had he. "What?" she asked, feeling very vulnerable. And warm. And giddy.

He stuffed his hands into his jeans pockets. "Everything you just said."

Laura slowly shook her head. "No. Not like that. Say it again."

Grant pivoted enough to see Vivian and Tucker, grinning to beat the band, and then turned to Laura. "I don't want to."

"Why not?"

"Because you...yelled at me about it."

"I did not."

"Did, too."

"I was not yelling."

"Were, too."

"I was not. I'd think I'd know if I was yelling, Grant."

"You were yelling." He turned, looking for witnesses. "Wasn't she? She was yelling."

Nods. Conferring glances between them. "You were. You were yelling."

"Da-da."

"Sorry, honey. You were."

"Ma-ma."

"That's what I heard."

"Butt."

Laura jerked a hand up. "Okay. I was yelling. But I meant it in a nice way."

"Good," Vivian announced, getting up from the stool. "Because I'm going to go get dressed and take this baby outside for a while. It's quit snowing. And babies love snow. So you two are on your own. Bye." She scurried away, taking Tucker with her.

Stunned by her mother's hasty exit, Laura swung her attention to Grant and felt her insides melting. He loved her. She hadn't been hearing things last night. He'd said it. And she wanted to hear him say it again. "I'm sorry, Grant. Really. Say it again, please? I promise I won't yell."

Grant let out his breath and met Laura's gaze. She saw the warm amber of his eyes go liquid. "I love you, Laura," he said.

She promptly burst into tears. And ran toward Grant. He grinned, and held his arms out to her. But she jetted right past him and ran out of the room.

DRIPPING WET, her clothes heavy and clinging to her skin, Laura stood in the guest bedroom, facing Grant, her back to the nightstand, the sleigh bed to her left.

"What's the matter, Laura? Was I wrong to say that I love you?" Grant made it a point to stay across the room from her, the closed door at his back, as if he weren't sure he should approach her.

Laura wiped her eyes and stared at the carpeted floor. *She* wasn't even sure why she was behaving like a teenybopper. "No. You weren't wrong, Grant," she finally said in a low voice. "In fact, I've wanted— dreamed of hearing you say those things. It's just that I..." She allowed her words to trail off. Because she didn't know what to say next.

"Is it because of ten years ago? You think I'll bail again?"

She'd thought it was. But she suddenly knew it wasn't. She really was over it, his leaving her back then. So she was honestly able to say, "No. And no."

"Good. Because I won't." The silence stretched out between them. "Laura, will you please look at me? Help me understand."

Biting her bottom lip, she looked into the face of the only man she'd ever loved. And her heart melted. His hair was tousled, his clothes wet, his sleeves shoved up. And he was still the most beautiful person she'd ever known. His warmth, his understanding, his humor. Why couldn't she talk to him? It was now or never. "I'm scared, Grant."

His amber eyes seared into her. "Good. So am I."

That surprised her. Frowning, Laura tilted her chin up. "You are?"

"Hell, yes. I don't know about you, but my life seems to be running on fast forward right now. Everything's hitting at once."

"Like what?"

"Well, like my father's heart condition—"

That took the starch out of her. Dismissing her soaked condition, Laura sat on the bed. She put a hand to her chest, over her own heart. "Oh, Grant. I'm sorry. I didn't know."

He exhaled sharply and sat next to her, leaning forward, his elbows braced on his thighs, his hands folded and dangling between his knees. He talked to the carpet. "We just found out ourselves. It's not too bad. Yet. It's one of those 'you better take it easy' things. But it means I have to take control of the family money. Now."

"Oh," Laura said automatically. Then the implications hit her. "Oh. Wow. So you don't work for the Tucker Company anymore?"

"No. Not as of yesterday. Which is why I've been hot on your trail. I had to find you. Because once I take over... Hell, I won't even have time to eat for about six months." He looked at her. Seriously. "And I wasn't about to lose you again, Laura. Not if it was in my power. Not if you...felt the same way about me."

Laura grinned, warmed by the intimacy of talking things out. This, more than anything else, was what they needed to do. And bless Vivian for knowing it and for giving them the time and the space. And bless Grant for what he'd just said. "So, you wanted me—what? In place in your life before you took over?"

A chuckle escaped him. "That sounds cold, doesn't it? But, yeah, something like that. Hell, I would have done anything, Laura. I just knew I had to see you. Touch you. It's like I was driven."

Laura slid her hand to Grant's thigh. "Good. I like that."

He sat up some, covered her hand with his. "You do, huh? But let me tell you, finally seeing you didn't come a minute too soon. Because I was supposed to sign all the papers yesterday—"

"Ah. Your noon meeting. But then the snowstorm of the century hit—"

"And it got canceled until next week. And of course, Tucker was already here. And Officer Hawkins and Ms. Gibson. And then Vivian. And my folks."

Stiffening, Laura gasped. "Oh, Grant—your folks. They're here in town. I forgot about them." Her next realization shook her optimism. "Aren't they going to be thrilled with this little turn of events?"

Grant held her gaze. "You mean about you?"

"Oh, yeah, Maguire. About me."

Grant took her other hand. "Laura, I don't care what they think. I'm thirty-two years old. I don't answer to them. I love *you*. I will always love you. I know that now. And I want to spend the rest of my life with you—" Laura's heart darned near pounded out of her chest "—if you'll have me. But I can't believe that ten years hasn't made a difference for my parents. If they can't accept this, you, then the hell with them."

Laura jerked her hands away and stood up. "Damn you, Grant Maguire. You don't even let me enjoy what should be the happiest moment of my life."

Grant pulled back, looking really lost. "What? I swear, every time I say how much I love you, I get yelled at. Or you break out in tears. Or go to sleep on me. I don't know what to do here."

So he did say I love you last night. Laura stored that in her heart and continued. "It has nothing to do with your loving me. It's about your folks. Are you just going to lay all this—me—on them and maybe kill your father? Like I want to live with that."

Grant shook his head, chuckling. "I hardly think it'll be that big a shock. Remember, they already know I'm here."

That stopped her. "Oh. Right. So...what do they think about that?"

Grant ran a hand through his sandy-blond hair. "I don't know. I didn't ask them. I'm more concerned about you. And what you feel. For me. And about Tucker."

Laura sat down. "Oh. Tucker."

"I know. What are we going to do about him, Laura? Damn, I love that little kid. How did that happen? I'm not big on babies. But he's different. And, you know, I really want to help him out whether he's with us or not. I've got all kinds of money. There's got to be something I can do."

Laura leaned her head against Grant's shoulder. "I know. I love him, too." She stared at Grant. "You don't mean...buy him, do you?"

Grant gave her a startled look. "No. Oh, hell, no. I meant...help him. Help his mother, his father. Somehow. I have an idea and want to talk with Ms. Gibson about it. But—and I know this sounds crazy—I'm not sure he has parents out there, Laura. I really think he's ours."

Could it actually be that he'd felt the same things she had? Laura hit Grant's arm. "Shut up. I know exactly what you mean. I fell in love with that kid the first minute I saw him. And you know me with kids. It's as if there's a big international symbol for No right across them for me. But it's like you said in the taxi last night. He *knows* stuff. It's as if he's here to bring us together." She sighed, slumping against him. "Oh, Grant. You're right. It's all hitting right now. What should we do first?"

Grant edged his shoulder up, bumping Laura, getting her attention. She sat up and saw "that look" on his face. A thrill raced through her, but she couldn't believe it. "Are you serious? I don't think so."

"I do." He leaned toward her, bracing his hand on the bed behind her. Which put him right in her face. "Why shouldn't we?"

Although she was completely titillated and starting to tingle in all the good places, she pulled back. "Because, Grant. Seriously."

He nuzzled her earlobe, traced nipping kisses down her neck. "I am serious," he said in a low, husky voice. "I've never been more serious in my life. We need to settle things between us first. Then maybe the rest will fall into place. So tell me you love me. Tell me you want me. For always."

Barely able to catch her breath, so very aware, in a way she never had been before, that her neck was most definitely an erogenous zone, Laura fought for words. "I love you," she whispered. "I want you. For always."

Grant slipped off the bed, knelt in front of her on the floor and wrapped his arms around her waist, holding her, wet clothes and all, his head against her heart. "Tell me you'll always be mine."

Laura embraced him, running her fingers through his hair. She cupped his jaw with her hands, tilting his head until she could see those black-lashed amber eyes of his. "I will be yours forever. I always have been."

Grant's wide grin narrowed his eyes, tilted them at the corners. He nodded, seeming to stare right into her soul. "Good. Then let's get naked."

With that, he jumped up and began peeling off his clothes. Despite the clinging wetness that fought him at every turn, he was tearing them off at a speed that was almost comical. Laura couldn't help laughing at him.

Until he stopped, half-dressed, and stared at her. "What's so funny?"

Without giving her a chance to respond, he grabbed her wrist and pulled her more-than-willing self up. And began helping her disrobe. It was no easy task, given the soaked and stretching condition of their clothing. But before too much was exposed, Laura gasped and stopped Grant's manic striptease. He frowned. "What?"

"I just thought of something."

"No. Don't tell me we're out of condoms. I'll shoot myself—"

Laura hit him. "No. Not that. I just thought of something I hate."

"Oh." He tried again to tug her sweatshirt off. "Well, tell me what it is, and I won't do it."

Again grabbing his wandering hands, Laura stared at him. "No. Not that. Not sex things."

"Then what?"

"The paparazzi. I hate them."

"Then we agree. Because so do I." His hands went to work again. He dove for her jeans.

Again Laura stopped him. "Grant. I am serious. They'll be crawling all over us, won't they? Once it's known we're an item."

Grant gave up. He decided to get back to his own clothes. "Yes, they will. I wish it could be different. But...welcome to my world. After a while, you don't even notice them. They're like gnats. Or mosquitoes." His zipper seemed to be stuck. Grant's knuckles turned white with effort. He stopped, put his hands to his waist and stared at her, his face like granite. "You know what? I'm about over this."

And suddenly, all their problems aside, Laura thought

that would be a tremendous shame. Quite wantonly, she stepped up to him, grabbed him by his waistband and pulled him against her. "Here. Let me try." She lowered her hand to his fly and cupped his...

Grabbing her hands, Grant sucked in a deep breath. "Okay. Move your hands from there. I'm serious— ouch. Careful. It's very sensitive. Come on, honey, we've got to—"

"Ye-es?" Laura said, snuggling up to him, rubbing herself against him. "We have to what, Grant?"

He stared at her. "Get you out of these wet clothes."

Laura burst out laughing. God, how she loved him. Impetuously, she reached for the neck of his sweatshirt and pulled him down to her. "Come here, you big sexy thing, you." And then, gripping the back of his neck with one hand, her other still fisted around his shirt, she kissed the ability to do higher math right out of the man.

When she finally took pity on him and broke off the kiss, allowing him to come up for air, Grant was blinking, gasping. "Damn. I don't...know what I...said or did to warrant that. But...whoopee for me."

"Yeah. I know. My toes are curled. How about yours?"

"Oh, yeah. Everything. My hair, my toes, my—"

Laughing, Laura put a hand over his mouth, stopping his words. "I think I know where you're going with that thought." Grant smiled. Then he licked her palm.

Startled, Laura screeched, jerking her hand away. Laughing, Grant caught her and rained kisses down on her face, her jaw, her neck... Reaching under the wet sweatshirt, his hands on her bare skin, he took hold of the lumpy material, and in one smooth move it was over her head.

The rush of air against her damp skin made Laura

shiver and hardened her nipples into tight buds. Grant's eyes widened, and he sucked in a breath.

"Oh, Grant," Laura murmured, feeling hot and drugged, her limbs liquid with desire as she tugged his sweatshirt off and stared at his chest. "Dear God, you're gorgeous." She focused on his square-jawed and handsome face. "But what about Mother and Tucker?"

He smirked. "I think they're gorgeous, too."

Laura had to laugh. "Not that. I mean, they haven't even left yet. They haven't had time to get dressed."

Grant jerked his hands to his hair, raked them through it. Laura almost died at the sight of his hard and contracting abdominal muscles, at the dark line of hair that thinned at his waist and… "Laura Elizabeth Sloan, what *is* your point? I am on fire here. If they haven't left, they will. Your mother's intention was to give us this time together, right?"

No longer able to blink, much less think, Laura looked at him. "Right. So why are you standing there talking?" She reached behind her back, worked the snaps and then—ta-dah—her bra came away from her body and went sailing.

Which made Grant catch his breath. "You are stunning. Wow."

Laura grinned, bare and proud, staring at him with want in her eyes. Grant returned her hot look until the distant sound of the front door opening and then closing captured their passion-drugged senses. "They're gone," Laura whispered, biting her bottom lip. "That means we're alone."

"Like you said, why are we standing here talking? You in?"

Was she in? Was he kidding? Faced with that chest? Those muscles? The way she knew they felt against her naked skin? "Oh, yeah. I'm in," Laura said, launching herself into his arms.

Grant caught her handily. Laura's legs went around his waist, her arms around his neck, and then, as one, they made their way, kissing, moaning, tasting, feeling, toward the big, already mussed sleigh bed behind them.

10

WHEN GRANT FINALLY, happily emerged from the bedroom with Laura, they were again wearing their wet—well, damp clothes. What choice did they have? The only clothes he had here were the ones he'd worn last night. And all her clothes were on the other side of the loft. And she wasn't prepared, she said, to go skittering naked across the open spaces to get to her wardrobe and risk getting caught by her mother, who'd most definitely give her a lecture on safe sex that would put Laura off sex for the next twenty years.

Grant wasn't willing to risk that, either. No sex for twenty years? No way! But for Vivian—with five marriages and five kids—hell, she needed to lay off the sex, as far as he was concerned. So here they were, dressed. Both of them barefoot. Laura braless. Him in his jeans and T-shirt. Her in her jeans and sweatshirt. Which she held out in front of her with her fingertips and a grimace so it didn't lay against her skin.

No, they weren't perfect. But they were happy, love-sated and ready to face the world. Or more precisely Vivian. Who should be back from her stroll with Tucker by now. But the apartment seemed disconcerting quiet. Surely Vivian hadn't kept the baby outside for over an hour. Maybe he was napping and Vivian was reading. Grant liked that picture. As he adjusted his damp clothing, he whispered, "You ready?"

"Yeah," she replied. "To be a circus sideshow freak, the way I'm chafing in these jeans."

Grant chuckled. "It's not that bad."

She wasn't buying it. "Oh? Then you step out there first."

Now he wasn't buying it. "I'm not going out there first. You go out there first." He nudged her forward.

She balked. "I am not. My mother already thinks we're nutcases."

"We are. But this *is* Vivian we're talking about. As if she can judge."

"I know. But still—for God's sake, it's my mother out there. And she'll ask us again about protection and safe sex and talk about movie stars. I don't think I can listen—"

Grant spun Laura to face him and steadied her with his hands on her shoulders. His heart picked up its pace, his mouth felt dry, his palms wet. What she'd just said. Laura blinked, swiped a lock of strawberry-blond hair out of her eyes and stared at him. "Laura, just now, we didn't…well, use any protection. Oh, hell."

Laura put her fingers to her mouth. "Oh, hell is right. This is my fertile time of the month, Grant. I think. Not that I keep up with it. I've never had reason to. Well, until now." She stopped, stared at him. "Oh, my God. What if I'm pregnant?"

Suddenly, Grant hoped like hell she was. He was ready. Ready to settle down. Ready to commit. To Laura. To Tucker. To future babies. Somehow the images in his head only made his heart sing all the more. "I hope you are—" That made Laura frown. "I mean, we are getting married, right? I did ask you…didn't I?" She shook her head. "I didn't? Well, will you?" She nodded. He exhaled in relief. "Good. Then, about a baby. It's your decision—"

"I want it. I do." As if to prove it, she raised her arms and put them around his neck. "I am a modern woman. I can have it all. Work. A family. And I'll make their daddy very happy he's a man."

Grant laughed. "Their daddy already is. And I bet Tucker would love a baby sister or brother, don't you?"

Suddenly, in a lightning-fast switch of mood, Laura stepped back from Grant. She looked stricken, lost. Grant's singing heart hit a sour note and began thudding with dread. "What? What's wrong? Second thoughts already?"

She shook her head but didn't say anything. She wasn't going to run away and cry again, was she? He didn't think he could take that. But then she stepped up to him and placed her hands against his chest, looking into his eyes. Grant noted the fears, doubts and concerns edging out the gray of her pupils. And wanted to die. "What is it, honey?"

"Grant, I love you. With all my heart and soul. I do. The fact that I want to marry you, that I want to have your babies, that I want us to make a life together only proves it. Until the last three days, I've told myself I wanted none of those things. And I didn't. Not then. But now I do. And I want them with you."

She'd just said everything he'd ever wanted to hear. But he wasn't happy. Because she wasn't. "Then what's the problem? I don't understand. Why aren't you laughing and booking a bridal consultant?"

"It's Tucker, Grant. See what you do? First you tell me you love me and then you say your father has a heart condition. I don't know how to feel. And now you ask me to marry you—" She stopped, looking stunned.

"Oh, my God, you asked me to marry you." She blinked. "And then you bring up Tucker. It's like a roller coaster out of control. I'm so scared."

She put a hand over her mouth, swallowed a couple of times, then rushed on. "I can't give him up, Grant. I can't. I feel like he's ours. I want to keep him."

"I do, too."

She smiled quickly at him. "I know you do. And I'm glad. But I'm afraid our being who we'll be—I mean, come on, you're practically royalty in America—just think of the endless publicity. The photographers. The stories. We'll have so much to deal with. What will the courts think? I mean, will we seem stable? And oh, my God, your folks. They'll be thrilled."

Seeing the panic in her eyes, Grant had to stop her. "Laura, I understand your concerns. We'll deal with them. Even my parents. I keep telling you, I don't think they will be the problem you think they will. Because right now, more than anything else, they want to lighten up and be grandparents."

She wasn't convinced. "You've said that. But I'll be the mother of their grandchildren. They hate me. Grant, I don't want you to cram me down their throats. And I don't want to come between you and them. I never did. But now, especially with your father's—"

He gripped her shoulders. "Laura, do you love me?"

"Of course I do."

"Then marry me and make me the happiest man on Earth. What my parents will or won't accept is on their heads, their souls. You come first with me. I think they'll follow. But if they don't...well, I can't help that. And neither can you. All we can do is keep the door open and see if they walk through."

Laura's expression softened. So did her rigid stance.

She stepped into his arms. "When did you get so wise, Grant Maguire?"

Grant folded her in his embrace, holding her damp and slender body as close to his as he could without actually absorbing her. "It was a slow process, honey. It took me ten years without you to come to my senses. Ten years I'm sorry I let go past. I've been a fool, running from you, from my heritage. Or my destiny, really, as silly as that sounds. But I'm here now, Laura. And I want things to be right between us. I want that more than anything else."

In that quiet moment, probably the only one they would have for a long time, Grant felt the need to add, "My family will come around, Laura. Because they're family. But Tucker's situation is going to be tougher. We've talked about keeping him. But...well, he may have a family out there. One that wants him back."

A wordless moment ticked by. Then another one. And another one. "Oh, Grant, could this be worse? Or better? I don't know," Laura whispered.

A sense of urgency suddenly seized Grant. He pulled back, holding Laura by her arms. "Honey, look at me. We will take each day, each problem as it comes. Together. We'll do this. I swear it. If Tucker can't be ours, we'll stay close to him. We will. I told you I have an idea. And I have the money to make it happen. You'll see. Tucker *will* be a part of our lives. Do you believe me?"

Laura stared at him, her gaze searching his face, seeming to delve right into his heart. Then she smiled faintly. "I do. But it's so hard...about Tucker, I mean."

"The real world is a tough place, isn't it? All we can do is butt heads with it."

"You're right." She exhaled. "Nothing worth having is ever easy. Or goes smoothly. So let's get started."

Now Grant patted her on the shoulder. "Okay. And hey, it's just your mother out there. Hell, she'll be thrilled for us. And as far as I'm concerned, whatever happens from here on out, we can face it. If we're together."

Laura squeezed his arm and returned his smile, her gray eyes shining. "I agree. I love you. And whatever the flak, bring it on."

INSTEAD OF T-shirts and sweatshirts, they should have had flak jackets. Heavy-metal flak jackets, was Laura's stunned and panicky thought as she stood in her living room and faced her mother, who sat in one of the two overstuffed and upholstered chairs that faced the sofa. Across from Vivian were…Grant's parents. Sitting next to each other. On the sofa.

That's right. Stanton and Muriel. The elder Magnificent Maguires. Whose eyebrows rose when she and Grant stepped into view. Yep. Dressed to the nines, the Maguires were. Chic and elegant and smooth. And staring at her and their son. Who was barefoot and garbed in a wet T-shirt and damp, clingy jeans. And standing next to the one woman in the whole world they hated. Her. Laura. In her own living room.

Which Vivian, now that she'd pivoted to see what had captured the Maguires' attention, obviously felt a need to point out. "Look who's here, Laura. The Maguires."

Sick to her stomach, Laura turned her gaze on her outlandish mother and croaked, "Yes. I see."

But Vivian wasn't done pointing out the obvious. "Your clothes still look damp. I'd think they'd be dry by now. After all, you two've been back there for more than an hour.''

Heat exploded in Laura's cheeks. At her side, she felt Grant shift his weight. No doubt, he fought a strong urge to flee. She knew she wanted to. But before he could, she grabbed his sleeve and held on, never looking away from her mother. ''Um, Mother, can we talk about this later?'' *And the fact that you didn't let us know the second the Maguires showed up, you traitor?*

Vivian sniffed. ''Well, I would've told you when they got here. But I didn't want to disturb what you were doing. And besides, I thought you'd hear the intercom buzzing. But I guess you didn't, seeing as how you were...busy.''

The embarrassed heat in Laura's cheeks increased, surpassing her shock that her mother had apparently read her mind. She was *not* psychic, dammit. ''Um, yes. We were busy—'' She felt Grant trying to pull away from her. She held on tight. ''We were busy... discussing the future.''

''That's right,'' Grant said as he tugged free of Laura's grip and calmly strode across the room to bend over and kiss his mother's cheek. ''Hello, Mother,'' he said warmly. ''You're looking well.''

Laura watched Muriel Stanton stroke her son's cheek and murmur a greeting. She didn't know whether to trust the warming of her heart or the guilt in her soul for possibly coming between them again. Grant straightened and looked at his father, who was now standing. ''Dad.'' Then he stepped back and said, ''You may want to sit down, Dad.'' Surprisingly, the older Maguire did. Then, sending Laura a this-is-it look, he addressed his parents. ''Laura and I *were* discussing the future.

Our future. Hers and mine. Together. I've asked Laura to marry me. And she's said yes.''

Laura's eyes widened. *Here we go.* And she was right. The Maguires gasped. Vivian cheered. And a wailing—of the baby sort—came from Laura's elevated, open-railed bedroom. Everyone looked in that direction. But only until the intercom buzzed. Then everyone looked in that direction. Then, for some strange reason, everyone turned to Laura. Who couldn't seem to move.

Again, Grant took over. "I'll get the door, Laura. You get the baby.''

"Baby?'' The elder Maguires catapulted to their feet. Their gaze found Laura's and riveted her in place. And rendered her wordless.

But not Vivian. "Oh, yes. You'll just love him. Tucker's his name. He's a doll. Didn't I mention him yet?'' Laura stared at her mother. This, the baby, she'd kept to herself? The doll screamed again. Vivian turned to Laura. The intercom buzzed. Vivian called, "Hold on. He's coming.'' As if whoever was downstairs could hear her. Then she turned to her shell-shocked daughter. "Get the baby, honey.'' To the Maguires she said, "You are just going to love him. We all do.''

And that was enough to send Laura running—stiffly, in damp jeans—toward her bedroom. Behind her, she could hear Grant talking into the speaker but couldn't make out his words. She couldn't believe this. On the one day the entire city shut down, she suddenly had a houseful of company.

But when she heard Vivian telling the Maguires how nice it was to see them again even if they did break up their son and her daughter when the two kids were in college and so in love... Laura nearly lost it. She grabbed for the railing and put a hand over her heart. Because her mother wasn't done yet. Wasn't it funny, Vivian continued, how things were working out now?

Laura wanted to die. Right there. But first, she had to see to Tucker—who was wearing the blue Tucker the Bear sleeper she'd found him in—as the sobbing little guy sat up in the deep drawer and held his arms to her, stuttering, "Mama."

Laura melted. "Oh, yes, sweet little love, I'm right here," she cooed. "Come to mama, darling. Don't cry. I'm right here." She picked him up and cuddled him close, inhaling the precious, warm baby scent of him. "I'll never leave you."

She realized what she'd said. And stiffened. *Oh, my God, I can't say that to him.* She looked at Tucker. He was quietly hiccupping and clinging to her. Happily. Contented. *Oh, my God.* He didn't hate her. He didn't. She'd done it! She'd quieted him, and she wasn't holding him upside down or anything. Laura swung around and hurried toward the steps that would take her into the living room. Grant and Vivian would be so happy for her. And shocked, no doubt.

But not as shocked as Laura was when she saw her newest guest. She stopped dead in her tracks. *No.*

Ms. Gibson. Tucker's caseworker. Laura gripped the nestling baby tighter. His little fists closed around her damp sweatshirt. *No.* Tears stood in Laura's eyes. *No.* But...yes. Even now, Grant, sober of expression but ever polite, was introducing her to his parents as he helped her off with her coat and invited her to sit. She settled in the chair next to Vivian, who immediately and without preamble launched into the woman's life history, telling the Maguires everything she apparently knew about the slender and now stunned and embarrassed woman.

"Now, Mrs. Gibson here—she's a missus, not a miz. Well, a widow, actually— Anyway, her husband was a policeman. He was killed in the line of duty. It's very sad. And she doesn't have any kids. She can't have them. But she loves her job. She just wishes there was more she could do for the children in her charge." Vivian turned to Grant, and said, "Honey, isn't there something you can do about that, with all your money?" Then she turned to the elder Maguires. "Oh, yeah—she has two sisters, too. And they could both use good jobs."

A suitably shocked and embarrassed silence followed, during which Ms.—no, the widowed Mrs. Gibson turned Vivian's sweetly smiling way. On the landing, as yet unnoticed by the gathering in her living room, Laura stood still with Tucker. Who raised his head, stared at Vivian and drawled, "Damn." Laura's jaw dropped.

"Now, how did you know all that?" Mrs. Gibson asked Vivian. "And don't say you're psychic."

"I am. But that's not how I found out about you. When I was out with Tucker this afternoon, we went into the coffee shop next door and ended up sitting behind you while you were having a heart to heart with your friend. Where is she, by the way? I thought her new hair color was great."

And like everyone else who dealt with Vivian, Mrs. Gibson coughed up the facts. It was easier. "She went home."

"Oh. Good," Vivian said. She turned to the room at large. "A cup of tea, anyone?"

No one knew how to respond to that. Or maybe they

just had their mental hands full wondering what was coming next. Vivian reached over to pat the poor exposed caseworker's hand and said, "She's a caseworker with the state. And I hope she's not here to take Tucker away."

"Take him away? Why? What has happened?" Muriel Stanton blurted, looking around the room. She rounded on her husband, putting her hand on his coat sleeve. "Stanton, there's a baby. Do something."

Stanton Maguire turned to his son. "Is that baby yours?"

All Grant could do was shake his head before Vivian spotted her daughter on the landing. "Look who's here, Laura. It's Mrs. Gibson. Maybe she can help you and Grant adopt the baby."

"Adopt? He's not yours, either?" Stanton Maguire asked.

Laura, too, only got to shake her head before Vivian cut in again. "I'm so glad you two kids are in love. And getting married. That should make things easier." She looked at Mrs. Gibson. "Do they have to be married to adopt?"

That poor woman shook her head—only to have Vivian cut in again. "Well, I didn't think so. But I wasn't sure." She turned. "Isn't this great? We're all here. And on such a momentous occa— Wait just a damned minute." It was the first time Laura ever heard her mother curse. Vivian rounded on Mrs. Gibson. "*Are* you here to take this baby away?"

Laura held her breath, waiting for the answer.

But Mrs. Gibson's reply was cut off, this time by a red-faced Stanton Maguire. "Will someone please tell me just who in hell's baby this is?"

Laura, Grant, Vivian and Mrs. Gibson turned to him. "We don't know who in hell's baby he is."

Stanton stiffened. Muriel put a hand to her pearl-draped throat. "Then what in God's name are you doing with him?" Stanton looked straight at Laura—whose brain promptly turned to mush—then turned to his son. "And what do you mean you're getting married? What is going on around here?"

From where she stood, Laura could see Grant's jaw clench. "I'll be glad to tell you what's—"

"Grant, please," Muriel interjected. She turned to her husband. "Now, Stanton, dear, remember your heart." She put her hand on her husband's sleeve, her patrician features softening, her dark eyes pleading. "Stanton, a baby. He's so precious. I would so love to hold him. Please. Grant loves Laura. And she's a lovely girl. We were wrong back then. And we both know it."

Stanton Maguire's jaw worked. The scene, for Laura, was almost too intimate to watch. Especially when the elder Maguire exhaled and seemed to slump as he covered his wife's hand with his own. "All right. All right, Muriel." The older man got up and moved toward Laura. She swallowed and looked at Grant, who nodded and offered a hopeful smile. Stanton Maguire stopped at the bottom of the three steps and stared at her. "Will you join us, please?"

"Certainly." Laura managed to croak the words out, carefully watching her step as she descended with Tucker in her arms.

When she reached the bottom, Stanton Maguire took Laura's elbow and turned her, baby and all, into his arms. And hugged her to him. Like he meant it. Even patted her back in a kind gesture. "We couldn't be happier for you and Grant, Laura. Ten years is a long time to be wrong. It's good to see you again.''

Laura couldn't believe this. *After everything you did to pull Grant and me apart? Just like that, it's good to see me? Ha.* But then she remembered she loved this man's son with all her heart and soul. And was going to make a life with him. She wanted him to have a new relationship with his parents. One she could tell Grant needed. So, if Stanton Maguire was willing to take this big chance, then, by golly, so was she.

And so it was that when her future father-in-law pulled back and smiled into her face, Laura was able to say, and mean it, ''Thank you. It's…nice to see you, too.''

As Stanton rubbed Tucker's dark little head and smiled at him, Laura looked past him to Muriel Stanton, who was holding her son's hand as he stood beside her. ''And you, too, Mrs. Stanton,'' Laura told her.

Muriel's expression all but crumpled. Laura saw her grip on her son's hand tighten. And noted that he squeezed back. ''Thank you, Laura. You're very gracious.'' She looked at her son. ''I just wish—'' She turned to Laura, took a deep breath and started over. ''What I'm trying to say is, we were wrong. About so many things. We know that. And we want to make amends, if we can.''

''Please,'' Laura said, hefting Tucker's weight. ''There's…well, it's all in the past. Let's just consider it bygones.''

Muriel's smile deepened. ''Thank you, Laura. And if you would, if you can find it in your heart…call me Muriel. After all, it appears we're going to be related. And I couldn't be happier.''

Laura smiled. "Me, either. And I can do that...Muriel."

It was a start. A beginning. A place from which to move forward. A healing moment with great promise. One best left alone.

If only someone had told Vivian. Into this beautiful moment, one that promised to see them through many bumpy times to come, no doubt, Vivian spoke. "See, honey? They don't hate you like you've said all these years. And to think I didn't want you to marry Grant because his parents were so uppity. Well, they're not anymore, are they?"

Trapped next to Stanton Maguire, Laura could do nothing but stare into the uppity man's shocked, wide amber eyes. So like Grant's. Laura couldn't stop herself. She burst out laughing...thankfully, right along with Mr. Maguire, who said, "I'll be damned if this isn't the strangest day I've ever lived through."

He turned from Laura and crossed to his son and wife. And took Grant in his arms, hugging him and affectionately pounding the life right out of him. Grant pounded right back, Laura noted, standing there holding her baby. *Her baby?* The warm scene cooled for Laura. As if they'd all read her thoughts, everyone turned to Laura. And Tucker. Laura looked at the little boy, who stared somberly, his blue-eyed gaze on Mrs. Gibson.

All heads turned to the caseworker. "I'm not here to take him away," she said quickly.

Emotional gasps, laden with relief, filled the room. Laura glanced at Grant, who released his mother's hand and came to stand beside her, putting his arm around her shoulders. Smiling at him, her heart swelling with relief and joy, Laura knew what she had to do. Ask the hard questions. She focused on Mrs. Gibson. "You're not taking him away now. But you don't mean for good, do you?''

She nodded. "You're right. Because I don't know what will happen tomorrow. But I've been thinking.... This baby *belongs* with you.''

Murmurings of agreement filled the room. But Laura had to be sure. "Do you think that can happen? That we—'' she nodded at Grant "—will be able to keep Tucker?''

"Tucker?''

"Oh. The baby. We— I call him Tucker. It's a long story.''

"I'm sure it is.'' Mrs. Gibson smiled. "Of course, Tucker's real parents could come forward at any moment. But I don't think they will. Usually in a case like this, they don't. Which means Tucker will have to go into foster care.''

Cries of protest filled the room, but Mrs. Gibson raised a hand. "There's no reason you and Mr. Maguire can't be those foster parents.'' Sighs of relief echoed off the walls. "It's a lot of paperwork, but—''

"But worth it,'' Grant cut in. "We'll do anything. Anything to keep Tucker. In fact, we'd like to adopt him.''

Mrs. Gibson smiled. "I think that can be arranged. I don't believe the court will have any problem approving you. I mean, you are the Maguires.''

Laura felt Grant's grip on her tighten. She met his smiling amber gaze. "Yes. We are that. We are the Maguires.'' Then he stepped forward to shake Mrs. Gibson's hand.

Overcome with emotion, Laura swung Tucker in front of her and held him up, kissing his little fat cheeks, then pulling him to her. Right side up. And without dropping him. "Mama," he shrieked happily.

Everyone in the room laughed, descending on Laura and remarking on the baby's rare intelligence. And how much he looked like...well, no one in this room, but Muriel thought he had the Maguire nose, and Vivian was sure the child had the Elderschmidt—her maiden name—psychic vision. Wait until Irving saw this one. Their first grandchild. And look at those hands, Stanton added. A pro quarterback's hands, no doubt about it. Laura happily showed the little boy off, like a little king. Tucker graciously accepted all the attention as his due.

And then, suddenly, Laura noticed Grant wasn't there. Immediately, Tucker said, "Da-da?" Surprised, but not really, Laura looked at the baby. He winked. She shook her head. Who knew with this kid?

Then she heard Grant's voice. But surrounded by Tucker's admirers, all she could do was crane her neck and try to find Grant through the crowd. She caught sight of him standing off to the side, talking to Mrs. Gibson. They were deep in serious conversation. Curious, Laura listened in. And smiled.

"And next week I'll be taking over the Maguire holdings from my father. I've been thinking about what I want to do with a portion of our liquid assets. Which is why I wanted your card last night."

Mrs. Gibson nodded. "Oh?"

"Yes. See, I'm thinking of starting a foundation, Mrs. Gibson. I haven't really talked any of this over with Laura yet, and of course she'll be a big part of it, what with her advertising expertise and her ability to get the word out there, but I want to call it the Tucker Foundation. And have it work for children like Tucker. And their parents. A fully funded, nonprofit organization to somehow help them. But I'm not sure how to go about it. This is where you come in.''

Mrs. Gibson looked at him. ''Me? What can I do?''

''Well, you can run it for me, actually.'' The woman pulled back, her eyes wide. Laura noticed that Grant went on as if he hadn't noticed. He should have looked ridiculous, standing there barefoot in wet clothes. But what he was doing was so noble it didn't matter. And Laura had never loved him more.

''Delineate the needs, things like that,'' he was saying. ''And someone like you, someone with experience should run it. I don't want any parent to feel they have to abandon their child out of desperation. I want them to have a place to turn for immediate help. For jobs, maybe. And medical help. And counseling. Food. Clothes. Things like that. I know governments have funds set up for this kind of thing. But why can't the private sector, too? What do you think?''

''I think I'm overwhelmed, Mr. Maguire.''

''Call me Grant. But do you think this is something you'd be interested in doing? I'll make it more than worth your while. And if you think your sisters would be interested, we'll bring them on board, too. But that'd be your call. As would all the employees.''

The former caseworker put a hand to her chest and smiled. ''Oh, yes, Mr.—I mean, Grant, I'm very interested. I know my sisters will be, too.'' She nodded in a gesture of respect and added, ''And by the way, I think it's a wonderful thing you're doing.''

Grant put his hand over hers. ''No, Mrs. Gibson—''

''Linda. Please.''

Grant smiled. ''Linda. It's a wonderful thing *you're* doing, helping us with Tucker the way you have. You have a lot of heart. And I hope you can continue to help us.''

"Oh, I think I can.''

A look of relief swept across Grant's features. Laura had to smile through her tears of joy. This little baby meant as much to him as he did to her. What a great father this man was going to make. "Good,'' Grant said. "Oh, one more thing. I don't want us to be considered on any other merit than our suitability as parents.''

Oh, no. Laura barely bit back a squawk as she separated herself from the crowd, and walked toward Grant and Linda Gibson. She gave Grant an overly bright grin and said through gritted teeth, "Can I speak to you in private a moment, please, sweetheart?''

Grant looked surprised. He smiled. "Sure.''

"Good,'' Laura announced, pivoting to hand Tucker to Muriel Stanton, whose eyes widened happily. "Will you take him, Muriel? I have to talk to your son.''

"I'd be delighted,'' she gushed, taking Tucker from Laura and slowly drawing him to her as if he were a rare and precious jewel. "Oh, my sweet little man,'' she cooed, her cheek next to his.

Tucker raised an eyebrow but didn't say anything. Laura exhaled in relief and took Grant's arm. "If you'll excuse us...'' And then she carted Grant off, chewing the man's ear—verbally—as they crossed the room. "Grant, did you just hear yourself?''

"About the Tucker Foundation? I was going to tell you.''

"Not that. By the way, I think it's a wonderful idea. And you're wonderful, too. I meant about us going through the adoption process on our parenting merits alone.''

"Why not? What's wrong with that? We're good—"

"Grant Leon Maguire. Think about it. Why are we soaked to the skin?"

"Because we were bathing Tucker in the sink and he— Oh."

"Uh-huh. And where does he sleep?"

"In a drawer. But, hell, Laura, I think we can afford a crib before the state pays a visit."

"And that's another thing. Where will the state be going to pay this visit? My place or yours?"

"Huh?"

They walked around the corner, out of earshot. And left the four remaining adults and one baby standing there. Vivian immediately took charge. "Aren't they the cutest couple?" After everyone nodded, saying oh, yes, they most certainly were, Vivian added "Won't they make great parents?"

Everyone sort of nodded, looked all around the room, but said nothing, really.

Not the least bit daunted, Vivian turned to Tucker and took his chubby little hand in hers. "So, sweetie, what do you think?"

Tucker grinned and pointed a pudgy little baby finger toward the hallway where Laura and Grant had disappeared. "Mama. Da-da," he said. And added a new word he hadn't used before. "Mine."

Look for a new and exciting series from Harlequin!

HARLEQUIN Duets™

Two __new__ full-length novels in one book, from some of your favorite authors!

Starting in May, each month we'll be bringing you two new books, each book containing two brand-new stories about the lighter side of love! Double the pleasure, double the romance, for less than the cost of two regular romance titles!

Look for these two new Harlequin Duets™ titles in May 1999:

Book 1:
WITH A STETSON AND A SMILE
by Vicki Lewis Thompson
THE BRIDESMAID'S BET
by Christie Ridgway

Book 2:
KIDNAPPED? by Jacqueline Diamond
I GOT YOU, BABE by Bonnie Tucker

2 GREAT STORIES BY 2 GREAT AUTHORS FOR 1 LOW PRICE!

Don't miss it! Available May 1999 at your favorite retail outlet.

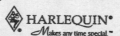

HARLEQUIN®
Makes any time special.™

Look us up on-line at: http://www.romance.net

HDGENR

LOVE & LAUGHTER™

Tell us a funny romantic story, we asked.

Jennifer McKinlay told a great one and won $1,000 in the Love & Laughter contest.

Up, up and away!

"Honey, when are we going to get married?"

"I'm not ready," Bob answered. Bob, my beau, my love, my commitment phobe.

After four years of dating and three years of cohabiting, this chorus and refrain had become our song. Feeling desperate, I consulted my backlog of *Cosmopolitans*. Sure enough, they stated emphatically to give him an ultimatum, but be ready to back it up. Oh, dear! Being a generous soul, I gave him one year.

The year ticked by. We continued our song, but now I had a new verse—"A ring or else." This did not have the desired effect of changing his tune.

Halloween came. I got bupkiss. Thanksgiving came. Nada. Hey, I'd have been happy to find a ring in my stuffing. Christmas came. I got a watch. Great, now I could really watch time pass me by. I gave up.

My beau is a quirky artist, and I knew I had to forgive his commitment-phobic ways in order to remain friends. And he is my best friend. So on New Year's Eve when he asked me to help him with a photo shoot at dawn, I agreed. Insane, I know.

Not being a morning person and suffering from the flu, I felt too lousy to shower that day. I slapped on a baseball cap and my best clothes-that-should-be-rags outfit. When we arrived at our destination in the middle of the desert, Bob went to chat with his client while I sat in our truck with a tissue up my nose, nursing my illness.

Upon introduction, I discovered that his client was a hot air balloonist. Ah! Now this made sense to me. Bob is petrified of heights, and I realized he was going to need me to take the pictures for him.

As the sun lightened the sky, Bob and I scrambled into the rising basket of our enormous red-and-black balloon. There were twenty balloons taking off around us, and I was snapping photos as if I was working for *Life* magazine.

Bob, poor thing, was too busy clutching the supports, his head tucked under the burner and a cap of ash covering his hair, to observe much of the view about us. Our pilot kept me busy with photos while he talked on his radio to our road crew below. (They follow you in case you crash. How thoughtful.)

We had floated for half an hour when Bob released his death grip on the supports to nudge me.

"Honey, what's that down there?" he asked, looking green.

I glanced down and darn near fell out of the basket. Our road crew had parked in the middle of nowhere and they were holding an enormous banner that read...

JENN, WILL YOU MARRY ME?

Being the rational woman I am, I yelled, "Oh, my God!" and snapped a photo of it.

"Well?" Bob asked.

"Yes!" I blubbered.

We kissed and hugged, and he pulled out the most beautiful ring I'd ever seen. It fit perfectly.

When I asked Bob later what had possessed him to propose in a hot air balloon, he said, "Because I wanted you to know that I meant it."

HARLEQUIN®
Makes any time special ™